Purity

Purity

Andrzej Tichý

Translated by
Nichola Smalley

SHEFFIELD – LONDON – NEW YORK

First published in English in 2024 by And Other Stories
Sheffield – London – New York
www.andotherstories.org

Quotation from the following sources gratefully acknowledged:
'Stairway to Heaven' by Led Zeppelin, 'Stairway To Heaven' by Dolly Parton, 'Turn!
Turn! Turn!' by The Byrds, 'Don't Feel Right' by The Roots, 'Dear God 2.0' by The
Roots, 'Eins. Zwei. Polizei' by Mo-Do, 'In Da Club' by 50 Cent, 'N.Y. State of Mind'
by Nas, 'Gallons' by Kojey Radical, 'ROCKABYE BABY' by Joey Bada$$.

1 3 5 7 9 8 6 4 2

ISBN: 9781913505981
eBook ISBN: 9781913505998

Editor: Anna Glendenning; Copy-editor: Bella Bosworth; Proofreader: Madeleine
Rogers; Typesetter: Tetragon, London; Typefaces: Albertan Pro and Linotype Syntax
(interior) and Stellage (cover); Series Cover Design: Elisa von Randow, Alles Blau Studio,
Brazil, after a concept by And Other Stories; Author Photo: Carla Orrego Veliz.

And Other Stories books are printed and bound in the UK on FSC-certified paper. The
covers are of G . F Smith 270gsm Colorplan card, which is sustainably manufactured at the
James Cropper paper mill in the Lake District, and are stamped with biodegradable foil.

A catalogue record for this book is available from the British Library.

And Other Stories gratefully acknowledge that our work is supported using
public funding by Arts Council England and that the translation of this book was
partially funded by the support of a grant from English PEN's PEN Translates
programme, which is supported by Arts Council England, and by a grant from the
Anglo-Swedish Literary Foundation. The cost of this translation was supported
by a subsidy from the Swedish Arts Council, gratefully acknowledged.

Supported using public funding by
ARTS COUNCIL ENGLAND

MIX
Paper | Supporting
responsible forestry
FSC® C171272

ENGLISH PEN

FREEDOM TO **WRITE**
FREEDOM TO **READ**

SWEDISH ARTSCOUNCIL

CONTENTS

OUTBURST

It all starts with the voice. *I'll kick your teeth in.* Then I see the man. He's walking up the gangway of the bus. He moves forwards, spitting out threats. I'm standing by the doors, next to a buggy. I've been at my mum's seventy-fifth birthday party and have brought away two big plastic bags full of fruit. Apples, oranges, pears, pomegranates, kiwis and grapes. I've put the bags down in between my legs, and now I push them closer to the side, carefully so the fruit doesn't tumble out, as I think about how he must be on the phone to someone. It's like I'm making space for him and his threats. But then I look up again, just as he's passing me, and see that he's not on the phone; it's us, the other passengers, he's addressing. Not anyone in particular, but everyone, and somehow no one. *You don't know who you're dealing with. A monster. I'll fuck you up. Get me? I'm a monster.* He's wearing a black T-shirt with a martial arts logo, DOJO-something-or-other, it says. He's short and muscular, with big letters tattooed on his forearms, but I don't catch what they say. I can only see the swaying, the neck, the big triceps. He's holding a pale grey bundle in one hand, a jacket maybe, or a sweater. *What are you looking at? I'll beat the shit out of you, get me, I'll beat the shit out of you.* Then I can't see him any more, I just hear his voice. I prepare myself for something but I'm not sure what. How far will he go? Who's going to intervene if he jumps someone? Is he armed? Should I risk my life for the sake of a stranger? I take a deep breath and suddenly feel horribly tired. It's warm on the bus. I note the play of looks — averted, curious, fearful, cautious. Lucky I'm getting off soon, I think. I'm not cut out for this stuff. And then the bus pulls in at my stop by Nobeltorget, without anything else happening. But when I've got off the bus, with my bags of fruit, I see he's also on the pavement. For some reason I don't leave, I just stand there, staring at him, along with two or three other people. A man shakes his head, an older woman says with a crystal-clear Eastern European accent:

'This is actual verbal abuse. This is actually an attack. You're attacking us all.'

He doesn't seem to hear anything, makes a few more threats, kicks the headlights and smashes the bus's big wing mirror with an advanced elbow strike.

'Not just verbal, now,' someone smirks.

The bus driver is on the phone.

The dojo guy walks off in one direction, I in another.

When I get home, I make coffee in the moka pot my brother gave me for my birthday, rinse some of the fruit and sit to jot down a few lines about the bus journey. It puts me in mind of the plot, so to speak, or the content, the events described, in Raymond Queneau's *Exercises in Style*. An encounter on a bus. A dispute, or some form of staged hostility. And then a repeat encounter. Wasn't that it? In ninety-nine different ways. Is that what's awaiting me? Ninety-nine different versions of getting my teeth kicked in? Is the monster going to beat the shit out of me? Am I going to bump into him in one of the doorways down here? Is he going to offer me drugs? Are we going to pass each other in a nightclub, stand there, heads bobbing, a few metres from one another on the dancefloor? Or am I just going to catch sight of him, in the distance, somewhere else? See him when he's in a completely different frame of mind. In the library, leant over a pocket calculator, glasses on his nose, with an orange pencil that he's twirling on his finger. With his kids in a playground. Tired and unshaven, his daughter's flowery jumper shoved into his back pocket and a grimy teddy in one hand. Or sitting with some friends outside a café, a cappuccino or a beer in front of him. Funny stories and laughter. Or maybe he'll sit next to me on the train tomorrow. We'll say a reserved but friendly hello and then fight, in silence and without touching each other more than is necessary, over the little armrest between the seats. That familiar old ritual. But at least he'll say *Excuse me* when he has to push past to go and buy a drink or go and take a piss in the little toilet where the paper's all gone and the floor is wet. His mum will call him. Maybe it's her he's going to see. I can hear they're speaking Albanian, but I only understand a few words, among other things *Të dua*, which means 'I love you'. I recognise it because I had a girlfriend once who was from Kosovo, and sometimes she used to say those very words to me. Valentina, she was called. I think about her and am struck by the fact I haven't seen her in sixteen years.

I slice a pear and cut a pomegranate in two, then I take a heavy wooden spoon and beat the kernels into a bowl. I still haven't learned that trick where you just cut into the skin and open up the fruit like a flower. Of course I get juice all over my T-shirt, it's always the way. Tiny little blood-red specks on the white fabric. I put the fruit down and watch the juice collecting in the lines on my palms.

Valentina. She told me she was named after Valentina Tereshkova, the first woman in space, but I don't know if she just made that up. I used to call her Valle. She moved to the US later, to study, something to do with biochemistry. I wonder how things went for her. Well, I guess. She was always so serious and disciplined, not like her brother Valon, who also got called Valle and who did a few stints for various petty crimes. But he sorted himself out after a while and got a job at a carwash on Norra Grängesbergsgatan. He threatened my life once because he got it into his head that I'd hit his sister. It was a misunderstanding, I've never hit a woman in my life. All this was in the early noughties. At that time, after 9/11, there was a lot of chat in my family about 'the Muslims', and I knew many people disliked the fact I was seeing an Albanian girl. Not that they ever said anything to me, they weren't confrontational like that. They didn't need to be, I could tell something was up. My grandma had suddenly started referring to herself as 'Christian' and wearing a gold cross she'd inherited from a relative. But I knew she wasn't religious, she probably hadn't set foot in a church since leaving Albufeira, a town in southern Portugal, at the end of the fifties, to live with my grandpa, who was a Russian sailor. They spent a few years in Holland in the sixties, then Germany and Denmark, and finally Sweden, Gothenburg at first and then Malmö. My grandma's brother and my grandpa's niece moved there with their families. Then Grandpa got cancer and died. The last few months he just lay around reading Joseph Conrad novels and Plato's *Phaedo* and seemed so elated and jolly people thought he'd gone mad.

The pear is hard and unripe. The pomegranate, on the other hand, is overripe; at least half the kernels are bad. I eat the pear anyway and start thinking about the time I drank freshly pressed pomegranate juice on the street by the Galata Bridge in Istanbul. I was there with Valle, her friend Sandra and my friend Bülent, who we called Bullet. We were hungover, because we'd been out dancing the night before. It was at a separatist gay club, with a women-only section. Bullet had gone off somewhere so I stood around drinking beer on my own for a while, then the girls came back to the mixed side and we danced to Destiny's Child and what I remember as hard Eurotechno, I can't tell you what exactly, it's not really my music. But I remember clearly: that pomegranate tasted absolutely fantastic. Then we ate some fish and started drinking raki again.

I sit down at the kitchen table and try to remember whether Beyoncé was in Destiny's Child, as I crush the kernels in the bowl. Then I drain the deep red juice into a glass and drink it in two or three gulps. I think about the people who were fishing on the Galata Bridge and I think about the Golden Horn, and the Bosphorus and the Aynur concert and how I'd suddenly, unexpectedly burst into tears when she and her band played an intense yet tranquil song.

I started sobbing uncontrollably and felt deeply embarrassed, because I realised I was disturbing the concert. I toss the crushed kernels into the food waste bag and think about the boats of the Bosphorus and about the mosques, about the little glasses of sweet tea, about Valentina's black hair, which she tied up in a big low bun while telling me she'd really like to take a walk on her own the next day.

Të dua, I say aloud as I sit at the table, and realise it feels like I dreamt all that, as though it never really happened. As though I'd made it all up, these Albanian words in Istanbul. Then I remember where the phrase came from and again I see the guy on the train before me. He feels completely real.

A while after he speaks to his mum, he calls someone – a friend, I guess.

'Hey, it's Dardan,' he says.

He turns away from me, in towards the window, but he's talking so loudly I can't help hearing every word. It becomes hard to concentrate on anything else and I regret not choosing the quiet carriage.

'No, listen, listen,' he says. 'Yeah. We were at the gym. Me and Blerim as usual. We did an evening session – it's quieter then, not so many people. Yeah, it was pretty late, so it was dark and so on, and it was just us and two guys we didn't know, but I knew they were fresh off the boat, like from Syria or Iraq or something, we'd said hello to them and stuff, chatted a few times, you know, and Blerim put some music on, like, some nineties gangsta rap or something, I don't know what exactly, but you know, it was pretty hard and so on, like, Wu-Tang or whatever, and don't say it, I know Wu-Tang's not gangsta rap, but like, you know what I mean, ah come on, stop it, and anyway, we're doing our reps, nice and chill, you know, and these guys are totally green, running round from one machine to the next, taking selfies the whole time, lifting here a little, there a little, then here again, yeah you know, curls by the squat rack, kind of thing, trying to look totally serious, and fiddling with their phones non-stop, and Blerim burst out laughing, and then suddenly there was a little skit, you know, one of those interlude things, between the songs, that was like some fucking murder or something, on the record I mean, like shots firing, shouts, you know, bitches screaming hysterically and more shots and like a load of furniture falling over, and bam bam bam, it's noisy as hell, chaos, you know, pure chaos, and the thing was, so like, I was sitting right next to these guys, and the thing was, I saw them leap up, and their eyes, like, it was panic, man, real panic, I swear, they looked over at the door, the windows, and you know it's totally black out there, completely dark, like a wall, you get me, it was only a few seconds, but I could see their pulses had gone right up, to like 150, 200 beats per minute, yeah, and then afterwards, when they realise it's only on the record, that it was just a *skit*, one of those interlude things, like, it was just on the record, it wasn't for real, that's when they start feeling a bit embarrassed, and the vibe gets weird, everyone laughs, what the fuck, chill man, and I said to Blerim afterwards that's the last fucking time you play that shit in there, you get me, and he agreed 100 per cent, there was no doubt at all, he'd seen it too, those looks, I swear man, it was no joke, you get me, something happened there, it was for fucking real, and to be honest, it's not something you can hack seeing day in day out, you know, it's like, not a look you want to see, I mean, like, maybe it sounds like ego or something, but that's just how it is, you don't want to be faced with that panic, get me, you don't want to be stand-ing next to someone who's feeling that panic, I mean, I don't know, that's just how it is, I mean, go ahead and shoot me, yeah, but I just want to go down the gym with my mate in the evening, cool, calm, do my reps, chat shit, wind down, you know, my job is stressful too, getting so much shit the whole time, so I need space, you know, a free space, where I can forget about other people's problems, you get me, so I don't want to have to take their panic, it's got nothing to do with me, you get me, I mean a man's got to fucking be able to listen to skits, really, a man's got to be able to listen to his interludes without some guy next to him flipping out, to be honest.'

Something like that. Then he starts talking about a competition in Copenhagen, some martial arts thing, I lose focus and start thinking about Valle again. Because I never cared what other people said about me, and us. I met my family occasionally, went to see Grandma, ate her fish soup and kissed her on the cheek and all that. And then I cycled back to Valle's. I didn't say anything about the disharmony in my family, but I think she got it anyway, because I never wanted her to join me on those visits. We mostly met at her place, watched films, drank wine and had sex. We slept in her stripy single bed, ate breakfast at the little kitchen table, which was full of her uni books and notepads. Then I usually smoked a fag out of the window before she threw me out because she had to study or go to Espresso House and work her shift. At that time I was mostly just hanging around, working part-time at the grocery store in Nydala, sitting at home, reading books and waiting, naïve and unfocused, for something interesting to happen.

'Why don't you quit?' I used to say.

'Let's pack this all in and move to Portugal and become fishermen.'

Or: 'Let's save up for a fishing boat and just take off.'

Or: 'Let's move to Kosovo and be farmers. Or English teachers.'

Neither of us took these words seriously, but somehow they amused us both for quite a while.

Several years after we broke up, I bumped into her, in a night-club on Stortorget. At first I was happy, but then I realised she'd taken something. I don't know what, I'm not good at seeing that kind of thing and I've never been interested in drugs, but I noticed something was up, you could see it in her eyes and in her sort of slurred manner. For some reason it made me feel really awful; I felt almost disgusted, nauseous. I don't know if it was jealousy. Maybe it was – I could see she was with some guy, some muscular, tanned guy who looked rich.

Hadn't he looked like the guy on the bus? Is that why I think he's Albanian? No, I don't know, they probably didn't look similar at all, it's totally improbable, really. Though sometimes I guess it's the improbable things that are true.

She looked at me with that drugged delight in her eyes and said, 'Good to see you.' I remember her emphasising the word *see* in a way I found odd.

Good to *see* you.

As though she needed drugs to see me. Or as though she'd been blind before, and it was only now, once it was over, once it was too late, once we no longer had anything to give each other, that she was, for the first time, really *seeing* me. I went back to my friends. They were partying – really going for it – in honour of Bullet, whose birthday it was, and who, what's more, had got a job with the EU and was moving to Turkey (in a sick twist, he joined a fascist organisation two years later, but that's another story). Later I saw Valentina on the dancefloor and started thinking about how we used to have oral sex, how I used to go down on her while I had two fingers in her arse and my thumb in her cunt. I don't know why these thoughts came to me, I didn't get turned on or anything, not excited in a warm or positive way, it just made me sad and my head felt kind of heavy. I tried to think about something else, but after a couple of hours I realised it wasn't going to happen and I told Bullet and my other friends I wasn't feeling great and was going home. Some of them offered to come with me, but I said it wasn't necessary, I was just going to go to bed anyway. It was good to get out in the fresh air so I skipped the taxi and the night bus, even though it was cold and quite a long walk. I thought the stroll would make me feel better and disperse the thoughts. But when I got home it just got worse. After frying two eggs and eating them with a baguette and some mayonnaise, then washing it all down with a few gulps of Prosecco that was left over from the pre-party, I snooped through Valentina's Facebook until I started feeling really sick and feverish. I must have been sitting there for a quarter of an hour, studying an image of the muscular, bleached-toothed tanning studio guy sitting in a shining black Range Rover, I was struck by such strong self-hatred that I couldn't hold back the tears. I slammed my laptop shut and got into bed. I'd been up at six that morning and now it was almost four so I fell asleep quickly. I don't know why that night in particular turned so weird, I didn't actually feel anything for Valentina – it had been several years, after all, and I'd already had two other relationships – but there was still something, there, something heavy, a surprisingly enduring pain.

When I woke the next day at around twelve, I felt better, despite the fact I'd dreamt of Valle in the night. It was a weird dream, sexual but also not. Almost anti-sexual. In the dream, she was criticising me for the fact that our sex life was bad, back when we were together, that she didn't come enough, that it 'revolved around your cock' far too much, even though I argued and said I didn't want to hear it, that she had this guy now, the guy I'd seen on the dancefloor of course, the Range Rover guy, who went down on her, and all kinds of other stuff that made her relax, and come, and so on. But that was exactly what I used to do when we were together. I went down on her and made her come, not infrequently several times in a row, even when she was on her period (at first she didn't want to let me do it when she was bleeding, but soon she realised it didn't bother me and she relaxed after that).

Or am I remembering wrong, I thought, am I just trying to convince myself that's how it was?

I look at my hands and see the juice has started drying.

I also remember waking that morning with Led Zeppelin's 'Stairway To Heaven' in my head: *Cause you know sometimes words have two meanings.* Then I realised it was Dolly Parton's version I heard within me, and that she'd added these lines: *If we listen and hold fast / To every question that we asked / The truth will come to us at last.* I wonder what it could mean? I thought. Did it have anything to do with the events of the previous night? With Valentina? As I recalled, there was a time when she listened to Parton a lot – 'Little Sparrow', one of the records was called, and there was that green one too, whatever its name was. I never got on very well with that music, that whole country thing, but apparently something had stuck.

A few years later, when Kosovo declared independence, I thought of her again as I saw the motorcade come driving up Bergsgatan with their Albanian and American flags. I stood there with Željko, an old friend from back when I played basketball. He was Serbian and he told me how a relative of his had had his house destroyed during the NATO bombing of Belgrade. He said that many civilians had died, that they'd bombed refugee camps and prisons as well, and that ethnic cleansing was now happening in Kosovo, thanks to independence. I remember thinking he was so calm as he talked about it. As though it was already ancient history, that it didn't have a bearing on us or anyone close to us. Not even when I pointed out that you had to understand their joy and their striving for independence, not even then did he get annoyed. He just looked at me with an expression that could, basically, have meant anything at all. That I was an idiot? That I was right, but that I was speaking in platitudes? That it was meaningless to talk about this stuff? Or that I had no right to an opinion, since my forefathers, both Russians and Portuguese, had been colonisers and imperialists? A heavy silence surrounded us. I looked at the Coke can, so tiny in his enormous hands. He swirled it and I heard the liquid sloshing about inside.

Now, as I sit here, recollecting these things, I start thinking too about how I once told Valentina about a sexual assault I was subjected to when I was eleven. It was nothing serious, but it was still an adult man touching me in a way that was far from OK. I'd never told anyone about it. When she found out about it, she was silent at first and then said I 'was maybe exaggerating'. She phrased it as a question.

'Maybe you're exaggerating? Bit drama queen to start talking about *assault*, no?'

And then she changed the subject. I remember feeling weirdly speechless and confused, I got dizzy and felt like a child. Or an adult who'd said something unfathomably stupid.

I hear again her drunken and somehow empathetic, warm voice, in the darkness of the dancefloor:

'Good to *see* you.'

Suddenly Dardan turns towards me. He's finished his phone call and holds up the phone.

'Excuse me,' he says. 'I noticed you've got the same kind. I forgot my charger. Could I borrow yours?'

'Course,' I say, after a few seconds' confusion. 'No worries.'

I give him the charger and we start talking about batteries, about our dependence on technology, about stress and frustration. He seems like a nice guy, so suddenly I say:

'Are you Albanian? I heard you talking before.'

I realise at once that I'm only bringing it up because I want to talk about Valentina.

He looks bemused, and says:

'Er, no. I'm not Albanian. I'm Polish. Or, half-Polish. But I was talking Polish just now, with my sister.'

'Didn't you say *të dua*?'

He laughs.

'No, what's that?'

Now I feel like I've made a fool of myself.

'Weird,' I say. 'I thought I heard it, and other Albanian words.'

'Maybe I was singing *Te Deum*.'

'What?'

'No, just joking. I don't know what I said. Weird that it sounded Albanian.'

'Yeah, sorry.'

'It's cool. I'm not offended. I've got nothing against Albanians, you know.'

'No, me neither.'

I hold out my hand.

'David, by the way.'

'Darek.'

We go on talking. He tells me about his parents, his Polish father and his Swedish-German mother, both dead for fifteen years or so. He talks about the final stage of the Second World War, describes how Poland's borders were redrawn after the war, how people in his family were deported and expelled.

'It's a long story, complicated, I barely remember it myself. Everything changes places in your head when you think about it.'

'How do you mean?'

'Well, I don't know, really. It's like . . . I don't think I can find a better way to describe it, really.'

'OK.'

Neither of us speaks for a while. Then he says:

'Or, it's like those optical illusions with the dots. The ones that disappear the moment you try to focus on them. You know the ones I mean?'

'Yeah,' I say. 'I think I know what you mean.'

'You have to look to the side, or you can't see them.'

'Yeah, I know. I know what you mean.'

'Yeah, you know. It's sort of like that.'

Our eyes meet and I can tell I've got a big smile on my face. He smiles too and shakes his head gently.

'And what's your background?' he asks.

I tell him briefly about Grandpa and then about Grandma and my Portuguese relations in Albufeira. About the beaches and the turquoise sea. He says he's been to Lisbon several times, that he likes bacalhau and port.

'And fado!' he exclaims. 'Fado!'

I laugh, mostly at this sudden enthusiasm, but he apologises, says it probably sounds clichéd, or touristy, to me.

'No, no,' I say, 'that's how it is. I like it too. My grandma used to listen to Amália Rodrigues as she crocheted in the evening. I used to lie on a mattress in their bedroom, I thought it was so cosy. You know, the crackle of the LP and Grandma singing along to certain lines.'

'I can imagine. It was such sorrowful music. Heavy and melancholic.'

'True. But she was proud of it. She and Grandpa used to fight, mostly for fun, but there was something serious behind it, about which nation's people had the most melancholic soul, Portugal or Russia.'

We laugh.

'OK. And who won?' he asked.

'Hard to say,' I reply. 'I don't know. They were both really cheerful people. They really knew how to enjoy life. But in some way it was also important to suffer well, if that's the right way to express it.'

When the train arrives at the station I tell him it was nice to talk, in spite of the little misunderstanding.

'Yeah,' he says, 'take care of yourself.'

'Same to you, my friend.'

We shake hands and go our separate ways.

I take the bus to the part of town my mother lives in, get off and walk towards her house. The sun is out and there's a festival on the square. Lots of people out, music, food smells, bunting. Something feels very wrong, but I can't put my finger on what it is. In the lift I stand very close to the mirror and look myself in the eye. I can't see anything special, nothing of note.

Pull yourself together, I think. Mum's turning seventy-five today and that's really something worth respecting, especially when you consider everything she's been through in her life.

THE USUAL
THOUGHTS

Every time I approach a car on a bend I imagine us colliding head-on. It's either me, veering over to the left-hand side of the road, or the approaching car – whose driver has fallen asleep or is drunk or is trying to commit suicide – that veers over to the right. Then, regardless of how fast I've been driving, I slow down so I'm going at just under eighty kilometres an hour, because I once heard a science journalist interviewing a researcher who said that the chance of surviving a head-on collision is violently reduced if the vehicle is travelling at a rate of over eighty kilometres an hour. Violently reduced. Could she really have said that? Or did she use the word *violently* to describe the slope of the curve in the graph that correlated *death* and head-on collisions? Or was it maybe *survival* and head-on collisions? I don't recall, but I often think about it, as I'm rounding the bend, preparing myself for a crash, for a head-on collision, for either *death* or *survival*, and wonder if this applies to both vehicles or just one of them, because if it applies to both it's over regardless, since no one, or at least as good as no one, only half-blind ninety-five-year-olds and anally retentive pedants, sticks to the speed limit on these seventy-kilometre-an-hour roads. Not even me, at the mercy of these thoughts and images every time I meet another car on a bend. On the straight sections I drive as fast as I can, and then I slow down again on the bends. I slow down and speed up, and slow down and speed up, and so it goes on, as though I were waging a battle, a low-key battle with myself. Then sometimes I think about my brother.

My brother, a critic and lecturer in literary studies, working in a field that, despite his anxious assertions, can only be described as an obscure part of an increasingly irrelevant, castle-in-the-clouds area of public life. He always says that all people, whether or not they are conscious of it, understand life as a battle between two sides. Between rich and poor, for example. Between men and women, labour and capital. Between reality and illusion, between devout and unbelieving. Or, in the case of intellectuals, between those who think and those who are incapable of mental activity. The ranks of the affected. Those who remain stuck in, as he says, ressentiment and reaction.

His words touch upon a discussion we've been having since our teens. Back then, it was a recurring ritual in which we playfully fell into traditional gender roles – probably a way for us to deal with the fact that we both, in various ways, transgressed these roles. Me as a mouthy, taekwondo-training 'tomboy'; him with his slender-limbed awkwardness and cerebral air.

'Hey,' I say then to my brother, since I'm not particularly interested in that game any more, 'the only battle that interests me is the struggle of common sense and good against idiocy and evil. Or, if you prefer different terminology, I might say the struggle of truth and compassion, or maybe of restraint and silence, of reverence and circumspection, of contemplation and prayer, of humility or even the savagely resigned grin, against the torrential and cascading verbal diarrhoea that pours forth whenever intellectuals set up their soap-boxes.'

And we go on like this, squabbling. But afterwards I often regret the harsh words. Because I know his superior attitude is just a role he slips into to hide his insecurity, his fear of dying alone, in some dingy room he's renting temporarily or in some equally dingy apartment he lives in alone, an apartment that reminds him of the seventies and the beginning of the eighties, when our dad lived in a so-called bachelor's hostel. Dad's neighbours made a big impression on us. They were all friendly, smiling and (in our eyes) big men. Most were alcoholics, addicts, mentally ill or troubled in some way or another.

And since then I've thought of all these tramps you see around as my family members, on some inaccessible, hidden level. I know it sounds pathetic and empty, but that's how I think and feel. It's not something I'm in the habit of talking about. Just like with those compulsive thoughts on the bends. My brother, on the other hand, he seems to harbour some kind of hatred for these fallen people. A hatred which is also self-contempt, of course. And fear that he too will fall, in spite of his academy and his World Literature.

'Don't be so afraid,' I say to him. 'What are you afraid of? Loneliness? Death? Or is it survival?'

My brother and I are sitting in my Volvo estate. Me behind the wheel, him in the passenger seat. We're talking. Nice and calm. Our relationship can be like this too. Kind, sensitive, empathetic. We're remembering our childhood, telling each other things.

OK, listen. Here's another weird story, he tells me. Remember I worked for a summer as an animal-handler's assistant? So, we were sitting there in his office. Some kind of basement place. I was sitting on this messed-up leather sofa and he was on the other side of the coffee table, on an office chair.

'Most people,' the animal-handler said, 'believe they're opposed to violence. But they're not. Not really. Really, there are hardly any pacifists. Most people are *pro* the monopoly of violence. That's the thing. Only the state is allowed to be violent, only the state can kill. And so on.'

We'd both finished our roast beef baguette with remoulade, and drunk a cup of coffee in the office. Lunchtime was almost over. It was my first day and he'd been going on like this since seven in the morning. He waved a pen in front of him as he talked. I sat on the sofa and listened to him. I had no choice. Like, he was my boss.

'And slaughterhouses, of course,' he went on. '*But that's just animals*, some dude always says. Well, well. You could say that. Sure. But I'd say to you: what is an animal? What separates you and me from a chicken, a dog, a horse, or for that matter, a cat from a pig? I promise, you start pondering these things a lot when you spend as much time with animals as I do. These days a lot of people have opinions on this and that when it comes to animals. Should you eat them or not? Should we keep them in, quote, slavery, and . . .'

He dislodged a bit of roast beef from between his teeth with his little fingernail as he talked.

'Well . . . take their . . . er . . . progeny, eggs, milk, and so forth. But that makes me wonder what they would say about people? It's almost impossible to buy an item of clothing today without a person having been exploited in some horrendous way, or electronics, do you have any idea how those damn gadgets are made? What people are forced to do so those metals can be extracted? You'd be terrified. But you can't say that. There are many things you can't say these days, in this country . . . well . . . you wouldn't believe it was true if I said it . . . if I told you what I've seen, and been involved in. You have no idea what people are capable of.'

'What do you mean?' I asked.

He looked at me like I'd insulted him.

'Nothing,' he replied. 'Never mind.'

'Have you ever hurt the animals?' I asked then. I don't really know where it came from.

'Are you thick in the head?' he said. 'The fuck you talking about?'

'I don't know,' I said. 'Have you ever hit them, or cut . . . you know, tortured them . . . I don't know. Or maybe not you, but maybe you've seen it? You hear about things, you know.'

'Alright, stop,' he said. 'One thing: I've been an angel, I really have. A patron. And them: my little heroes. My main characters. Every single one. Bull and mouse. Goat and canary. The whole bundle, yeah. The whole fucking menagerie. So shut your mouth.'

'OK,' I say. 'Apologies.'

Break time was over. We got up. He filled the water bottles and I carried his bags to the van. It was hot as hell.

When we got onto the motorway he started talking again.

'Sorry I lost my rag,' he said, 'but it was a bloody weird question.'

'Yeah, sorry,' I said. 'I didn't mean anything by it.'

'But you see, beasts . . .' he said. 'We're all beasts. Regardless of . . . composition . . . or whatever you'd call it . . . form.'

I nodded. Then something weird happened. I heard his voice inside my head and I looked at his lips but they weren't moving. This is what I heard:

'I think about animals more than people, I'll admit that. That's how it is. In various ways. I'll give you an example. Imagine I'm eating a pear. I'm standing there, over the sink, eating an overripe pear. A bit of the pear seems to be rotten. The rotten flesh, the taste of rotten fruit, makes me think of horses. Horses getting drunk, wild horses eating rotten, fermenting fruit and getting drunk.

'Wild, drunk horses, do they exist somewhere? I think, over by the sink.

'When would they have existed?

'Have they ever existed?

'I've forgotten everything I've learned. I'm standing there, bent over the sink so as not to drip on the ground, with the pear which is ripe and has started rotting, and the taste is full, rich, and insistent, strong and sharp and yet still rounded, I see a wild mouth, a horse's mouth . . . I'm standing there leaning over the sink with the pear, the overripe fruit, in my hand and thinking about a horse's mouth, about the brown-flecked teeth, the dirty-yellow, oblong, pale-brown teeth, about the pink gums, those firm gums, about the ruffles on the soft palate, about the uvula.

'Do horses have uvulas?

'I've forgotten everything I've learned about anatomy. Forgotten my zootomy. I guess pigs have them. Yes, pigs have them and people have them, but do wild, drunk horses have soft palates and uvulas?

'The horses are squealing and I'm leaning over the sink. I'm think-ing about different animals' mouths and this gets me thinking about the digestive tract, this, like, system of organs, that goes from the mouth to the anus and I wonder if this is the essence of a human. The rest – bones, muscles and skin – is irrelevant. We're not drunken wild horses. Humans – even I, leant over this stainless-steel sink – are no more than this flesh that's there in order for the digestive tract to exist. Right?

'The flesh on our legs and the flesh of our bodies, the flesh of our arms and the flesh on our hands that brings the flesh of the fruit to my mouth, the overripe, rotten pear, that tastes of drunken wild horse's dreams from an abandoned orchard in the Middle Ages. I guess there were icons there. I'm sure of it.

'But who is the patron saint of wild horses?'

This last question came from his mouth.

There was a silence.

'I don't know,' I replied, confused and unsure of what had just happened.

'No,' he said, 'me neither. We'll have to google it later.'

Another silence.

'Shall I do it now?' I asked.

'No, forget it,' he said. 'It doesn't matter. We'll be there soon. You can get the syringes ready in the meantime.'

'OK,' I said, getting out some bottles of ketaminol.

I decided I'd hand in my notice before the day was over. There was something aggressive and unpredictable about him that I couldn't stand. Was that why I was starting to imagine things? Or had I come down with something, got a fever? I felt my forehead and the back of my neck, which were both damp with sweat. Impossible to tell when it was this hot. It was as though everything had a fever. I took a few gulps of my water, which was already a little warm.

We sat in silence. For a while it seemed to me he was completely immobile, which made me nervous, but then I saw that he was making tiny little adjustments to the steering wheel the whole time, and then I saw him blink and I calmed down.

'Uvula,' he said. 'What a strange word.'

At first I had no idea what he was talking about. Had I missed something? Then I realised he was referring to what I'd heard him say just before. With his mouth closed. So it had actually happened.

'Yeah,' I said.

I visualised the word while I had another drink of water. For some reason my brain wanted to break the word down into three parts.

UV-U-LA.

At once symmetrical, and not, I thought.

'Right?' he said, excitedly. 'Pretty weird. You don't think of it that often. But it's important to think about these things too. I mean, the things we don't often think about.'

'Uvula,' I said. 'Yeah, you're right. It's pretty weird, it really is.'

'Hey, that's putting it mildly,' he laughed. 'Uvula, uvula. Uvula, uvula. Just think: you have your own uvula, right there in your throat.'

'You do too,' I said.

'It's true,' he said. 'Like the glans of a clitoris, hanging right there in your throat.'

'Or a single mini-scrotum,' I said.

'Like a stump,' he said. 'Just a drop of flesh. A tear.'

'Yeah, it's weird,' he said, parking the car. He stepped out and slammed the door shut. I started giggling uncontrollably, which made me feel quite ridiculous, though in a positive, relaxed way.

Maybe I would be able to put up with him, after all?

We carried the stuff up some steps. He pressed the bell, grinned widely and said: 'Here we come with our uvulas.'

My brother and I are sitting in my car, having a good laugh about the animal-handler and his jokes.

'Christ, what a character,' I say, as I become aware of the traffic posts rushing past rhythmically at the edge of the road, one after the other after the other for all eternity. I have to stop thinking about them, I think.

'OK with you if I smoke?' my brother asks.

'Course,' I say. 'Just wind down the window.'

'Dad's drinking again,' he says after a while.

'Yeah. I know,' I reply. 'He called me the other night, but I didn't answer.'

'It's fucking tiresome.'

'Yep.'

'And Mum's just constantly banging on about her keep-fit and how great she feels.'

'Well, yeah, but that's better than when she was ill, no?'

'Sure, but still . . .'

'What do you mean, *still*?'

He doesn't answer. His eyes are fixed on some point on the horizon. The traffic posts again. Oncoming vehicles. The roads.

Patterns unfold.

We take a break, stretch our legs. Petrol, toilet, snack. I spend a long time watching a bunch of gulls having a wild time in a half-covered skip. Interesting cloud formations above us. My brother talks – ironically, I assume – about the poetic potential of headlines.

'It's interesting, too, that it's never really news,' he says. 'Those words only ever reinforce what we already know. They are comments on a death sentence we've already been given. Just like everything else.'

'Yeah,' I say, 'maybe that's true. Nothing new under the sun.'

He bursts out laughing.

'That's what I mean. Now you're quoting the Bible too.'

I laugh along with him.

'Really? I didn't know.'

'Ecclesiastes,' he says. 'I have seen everything that is done under the sun, and behold, all is vanity and a striving after wind.'

'Aha.'

'Yeah. Even the pursuit of wisdom is a striving after wind.'

I don't say anything but I nod at him and think perhaps he's more insightful than I thought.

We sit in silence for a while and then walk towards the car. He starts humming and sings:

'To everything, turn turn turn / There is a season, turn turn turn.'

I feel energised. I drive out onto the motorway again and tell him about my MMA training, about different techniques, grips and throws, and it ends with me trying to describe how it feels to kick someone in the head. He listens, concentrating. Genuinely. Then he tries to explain to me the difference between *science fiction* and *speculative fiction*.

He smokes another cigarette. We talk about our half-brother who lives in Holland, in Nijmegen. It's probably fifteen years since we were last there.

'*Half-brother*, what kind of fucking word is that?' I say.

I come off the motorway. My brother throws out his cigarette butt and winds up the window. We turn onto an A road. I'm driving at 110.

'The traffic posts,' I say.

'What about them?'

'What's the distance between them?'

'Well . . . I don't know, what could it be . . . fifty metres?'

I think that that seems about right.

'Do you know why electricity sockets have two holes?' I ask.

'Electricity sockets? Which electricity sockets, what are you talking about?'

I see a truck coming towards us, the road curves to the right.

I accelerate and drive straight ahead. The front is enormous, I think. A row of horizontal black lines.

I'm probably thinking the word *grill*.

I read the word SCANIA.

I hear my brother's voice and I feel an enormous joy surging up from my stomach through my whole body.

I feel like laughing at him, at myself, at all this fear, and at how normal everything feels, in spite of everything.

THE RUNAWAY

They say people are happier when they're thinking about what they're doing, rather than when they're thinking about something other than what they're doing.

The runaway is a person who is thinking about running away, and she is not happy.

You see, the runaway realises that she is a person who has mistaken coldness for warmth and darkness for light.

Particularly the warm, yellow light in the room where I died, she thinks.

And then: hang on. Died? Lived.

The yellow light in the room where I lived my final days, where I lived with my thoughts and images, my thoughts and voices and memories and images.

Yes, she lived with thoughts and voices and memories and images and she has mistaken darkness for light in a room, in a yellow room, a dark room, a room of death, that is, a room of life. It's where she lives still.

In this room, all the other people are staff. In this room, everyone wears white tunics, togas, chemises. In this room she can think a lot but she can't do much. She looks out the window and thinks of the colours.

She doesn't want to mistake them. She looks at them and names them. One after another. At night she sees a yellow glow coming from the floor. Then she studies the shadows on the ceiling and tries to avoid thinking as well as doing.

She lives, you see, in a room of death where all the other people are staff. They come and go as they please. She tells them about her mistakes and about the colours and about the unease but of course she doesn't say anything about her thoughts of running away. One staff member asks if she'd like to make a colour wheel.

What's a colour wheel? asks the runaway.

It's a circle with segments in different colours. You can spin it and it looks like everything is flowing together and changing places. But don't worry, the colours are still there.

Yes, says the runaway. I'd love to. Let's make a colour wheel.

Then the runaway sits with her colour wheel and spins it and watches. It's impossible to name the individual colours now. She wonders if that's what happens with her mistakes: everything is spinning and changing places so quickly she can no longer tell one thing from the other.

The runaway knows nothing but the staff tell her everything. And then she can't let go of what the staff have said. Everything they told her about her life. About her parents, her siblings. Her parents who abandoned her, her new parents who ignored her, and her siblings, who tormented her and wounded her. The runaway has so many questions. She asks and they answer. Or she asks and they dismiss her questions.

Then one staff member grows tired of her. The staff member says:

PTSD is coming for you. The psychosis is coming, fuckgirl. Look, the piss is coming. It's classical conditioning, my friend. You want me to console you? You know what, no, I don't have time, I have to go and watch YouTube.

The runaway is thinking of running away. The runaway thinks that someone might be looking at her. Watching her, as if in a film, reading her, as if in a book, thinking of her, as if in a dream. Then, perhaps all this would have some meaning. The runaway is thinking of you.

The runaway is thinking: I know this is anxiety-provoking to listen to and that you can't be bothered to listen and that you don't get anything out of listening to this and blah, blah, blah. Yeah, I know. But still.

To begin with she knew nothing, but now she knows everything about how they left her there. Piss-soaked and alone in the yellow room, when she was three years old. The room with the yellow light. The same light, the same light as in the room with the staff.

She shouts and rages. Her lips against the cold letterbox. It is quiet on the other side. It must be autumn, the leaves falling down onto the street, they really are drifting down, just like in all your bad poems, she thinks. Irregularly, you know, but still straight down, the colours are wonderful, the children are lovely, really *enchanting* out there, death is exquisite out there, the melancholy is intoxicating and atmospheric.

In here, in this cardboard carton, in this sealed box, there are no colours, and not a sound can be heard. Nothing moves either, however much we jump and kick and shout, she thinks.

And then: what is this we? I.

It's a recycled image, you've seen it before, everyone's seen it. The staff are brutal. They remind her she has no home and no family. Nothing but yellow piss in an empty room and then they knock out her teeth and then they laugh at her and then she dies. How easy it could be. And out there is a silent, still, empty carton. A sealed box. It's impossible to care. Then the axe in the door, then all the cutlery in her head. So they'll see. So that maybe they'll see. And then maybe it'll be OK.

No, it's not going to be OK. She really wants to run away.

You see, she's mistaken loneliness for love too. Far too much has been too little. She's wasted time on fleeting, ephemeral things, she's wasted time because she's mistaken time for movement, or time for similarity.

My time is my enemy, she thinks.

It's my own fault, she thinks now.

She's learned so much. From the staff, from life, from the rooms that are different, yet similar. And nothing was as instructive as enmity. She'll definitely be taking that with her.

Even at birth she was her own enemy. The enmity followed certain patterns, they showed themselves and concealed themselves.

Showed themselves and concealed themselves.

She's made a list:

1. Birth. 2. I am one, two, three years old. 3. I am six years old. 4. I am ten years old. 5. I am thirteen years old. 6. I am seventeen years old. 7. I am twenty-five years old. 8. I am thirty-seven years old. 9. I am forty-nine years old. 10. I am sixty-three years old. 11. I am eighty-eight years old. 12. I am dead.

She is a dead woman talking and it's a mixture – of life and death – that is totally feasible.

You see, she hasn't only mistaken coldness for warmth, and darkness for light, and loneliness for love, she has also, repeatedly and for extended periods, mistaken life for death, and mortality for life.

Even the fact that I'm daring to give voice to all these abstractions, she thinks, that's absolutely bloody incredible. It's as though the conditioning isn't working.

To show is to conceal, and to conceal is to show. Evidence of this can be found by closing your eyes, by being dazzled, by fumbling, and through touch. That's what she thinks.

She thinks: what can I do, to be able to do what I'm thinking of?

Then she says out loud, to no one in particular: 'Or am I already doing it?'

She speaks death but no one hears. Her voice is smaller than her hands, and her hands are minute. She turns in every direction to show people that her mouth is in motion, but of course they're not even there, the people, so they can't see. When she says *them*, when she says *person*, she means her parents and siblings and neighbours and friends and the people who loved her or said they loved her – she doesn't mean the staff.

What are you thinking about? Are you thinking about your friends, your neighbours, your siblings, your parents? Don't do that, she thinks. This is not about you.

They say they love her but they hurt her. They harm her and say they want to live with her for the rest of her life. The irony of it, she thinks. You couldn't articulate the threat any more clearly.

And anyway, she's already dead, in that piss-yellow darkness. She's still a woman, thus far – hairy cunt, breasts and all. That goddamn blood. She's a woman who knows very little about this milieu. Death's milieu, death's environs. This too is life. She can feel it. It feels sort of warm and cold, soft and hard, weak and strong. The light blinds and the darkness conceals, there's nothing strange about it, it's perfectly normal, perfectly ordinary. It's an order of a kind.

Some things seem uncontroversial. Like the fact that there's a flickering on the inside of her eyelids. That the day is followed by night. That a stone falls and gas rises. And that those close to her talk about her behind her back, over her grave. *After* her life. Everything they say. She was sick in the head, the little bitch. We're rid of her now.

She dreams herself back there. The letterbox is cold, tastes of metal, the smell is a vague stairwell blend. The sound of cops walking up the steps with their fucking stuff. Piss and blood and she just hopes they're not hitting children. They take her and push her down into the carton and the carton becomes yet another room.

So many rooms, so many rooms at once, with thousands of branches, like an enormous birch tree behind the building. The trunk, the crown, the hanging-down towards the ground. She hears them call and she hears them shout. She almost kisses the letterbox, the flap that gleams and winks and leads the way out of the grave. The sound is on the other side. *Noise*, she calls it, but they can call it life if they want. Her life, on this side and that side of the grave.

Her life in pictures, long series that depict causal sequences. The pictures are common, kitsch and cheap, like sitting in front of the television on an ordinary weekday evening. People doing whatever. Inhuman things too. An angel breaks open the door of hell and vomits out a tide of fire and lava that sweeps away the whole of your evil world, all pain courses away. It's the most beautiful thing she's ever seen, the greatest pleasure she's experienced.

She is constantly searching for the simplest word to fit her thoughts and feelings. The thing that hurt is gone. That's nice, it feels good.

You're searching for a logic you can recognise, she thinks, that reminds you of yourself. But do you really think you're familiar with all existing logic? Are you really so dumb and delusional? You want me to tell you about violence and the consequences of violence. But can you imagine that the consequence of violence is not being about to talk about the violence, or the consequences of violence. Imagine that the consequence of violence is not even being able to see the violence, to make it comprehensible, to point at it: it's not even possible to say *violence* without being ashamed, and dropping everything and falling.

And being caught by the staff.

And then escaping.

I carry with me that hanging-down towards the ground.

I carry with me the words, the curses, the slang.

I carry the rage of angels.

All those cop people will be consumed by the flames of hell for what they've done. And for what they didn't do when they should have done something. All the state's representatives will crawl in the lava and be eaten up from the inside by red-hot demons.

Must I summarise it all again? she thinks. The animosity?

She makes another list:

1. Birth – this is self-explanatory (from my perspective, not my mother's), there's nothing more to say about it. 2. I'm one, two, three years old and we flee from something awful and I understand nothing and I don't know where I am. 3. I'm six years old and the adults say

we're going to die soon. 4. I'm ten years old and I'm still alive, but the adults just lie there staring up at the ceiling, so I have to make my own food and wipe my little brother's arse. 5. I'm thirteen years old and I fall in love with the rush of dissociation, it's the first time I feel safe. 6. I'm seventeen years old and grown up and happy and in love and violent and I have hundreds of friends and we live in great safety. 7. I'm twenty-five years old and strange things start to happen, I understand nothing and it's like when I was three years old and we fled and I didn't understand anything and didn't know where I was, except I'm twenty-five years old and I can't flee and I understand everything and know exactly where I am. 8. I'm thirty-seven years old and I realise I've been a child this whole time. I get to know this doubling: I know and I don't know what I am and where I am. 9. I'm forty-nine years old and I think it will be over soon and I wish it had been over long ago but my life just keeps happening and the dissociation keeps happening too. 10. I'm sixty-three years old and the dissociation continues and things feel awful because there's so much, so very much I regret. 11. I'm eighty-eight years old and now things feel good because it's almost too late for anything. 12. I die at the age of eighty-nine. I'm dead. A phantom, a spirit, or a ghost. I don't have the words for it.

She thinks: I understand that it's hard to listen to a ghost, the talking dead, someone who never says things that are fun or exciting or easy, that make you feel like a smart, productive, good and lovely person with a gut full of good bacteria. Or wait, sorry, you're not like that, you're different, sorry. You're too clever for that stuff. You know how to appreciate boring, difficult, awful things, and feel no need to be productive, lovely, or bright, so to speak. But still you don't want to listen, or you do want to listen, but you don't want it to go any further, if you see what I mean. But we must go further. Because I need you. I'm going to escape and you're going to help me. I'm going to use your body – your eyes and your mind – to go onwards and upwards, out, into the light. You're searching for yourself in these words and that's how I'll escape. I'll think, act, and be happy. I'll attack you as you sleep, from within, like a demon, at body temperature to begin with, then getting warmer until I'm red hot. The pain won't go away.

I'm not a ghost, not the talking dead. I'm a living being, playing dead. A mask. My living face pulses under the death mask. I'm at least as alive as you are. Do you really believe that the dead would waste energy on the living?

You'll be my way out, she thinks. Imagine that. And it makes no difference what you're thinking or feeling, or whether or not you believe in transcendence or whatever you call it. I'm already inside of you. The runaway, you call me. Take a stance on that if you can. Anticipate clarity in the light of that, if you can. You don't know what fear is. But one day you'll know. You think you know but you don't know. I'll take it with me. One day you won't recognise anything at all, absolutely nothing. I take this with me as I leave the room of death, the staff and the confusion. I take with me everything I carry within me. I take with me the hanging branches of the enormous birch tree outside the hospital window, and I take the memory of the staff singing 'Sleep, You Little Willow Young'. And I take with me the image of a colour wheel. I take the spinning of the colour wheel, and its colours that are still there.

STRENGTH
AND UNITY

'The painful deformation of human beings under the impact of destruction contradicted the Party's view that the fighter had to keep his strength and unity in any situation.' These words were spoken in 1959, in front of VEB Elektrochemisches Kombinat in Bitterfeld, outside the gates, under the large metal sign with its three smoking chimneys enclosed in a hexagon. I remember we hung around for a long time after the conference had ended, full of puppy-like joy, giddy with confidence, intoxicated by this new vista of clearly defined Sozialistischer Realismus that had opened up. Accompanied by our older, established comrades, we would now step into reality, into authenticity, into the day-to-day lives of the workers, into their greatness; yes, we would become one with them by systematically and conscientiously bridging all distances. And a new culture would take shape in East Germany. I can no longer recall the name of the person behind that phrase, and perhaps it's irrelevant. Perhaps it's just as immaterial as the name of the party that person once represented, as the circumstances out of which that statement arose – which is to say, politics – as my role in it all, as my story and the way it developed over time. I will leave all that to the devoted hacks and essayists your reality is crawling with. Nevertheless, now I have been asked to recount the details of my crime, this phrase comes to me and gets in the way of the chain of events I have set out to depict. The distance between words such as these, the epoch they are a part of, and the place where I now find

47

myself – a prison cell of the utmost materiality – is enormous, not to mention unbridgeable, and yet still they show up, like ratchets, wedged into the thoughts and memories I'm attempting to formulate. It means I must make a diversion here. I must, I fancy, speak as my victim, I must assume the role of the mutilated, I must speak with his voice and communicate what he sees, otherwise there will be no story, and, people tell me, without a story there will be no atonement. Whether this disguise really is effective, or if it's merely the desperate mimicry of a tormentor, is for somebody else to decide. The mutilated man is himself unable to comment on the events, is not able to contribute his own interpretations, recollected imagery, and references to sensory impressions, but were he able to say something on the subject, I believe he would begin his account with the statement that the whole thing took place in a house on Kungsgatan, in November, that it went on for several days, that it was opposite the fire station, that it was in Karl's apartment. Yes, he would say, it's a little muddled, my memory, but not far from there was a – what would you call it – a garden, maybe. During the day teenagers sat there kissing, and at night rough sleepers lay on the dark green benches. That is to say, that's how it was in the spring and summer, but not in November; now the beds were black and empty, with the odd leaf blowing around between the benches. Though perhaps all this is unimportant. The important thing, he would say, was that I wanted to go and see Karl, in his apartment. We'd been friends a long time, since childhood actually. I was actually supposed to be leaving the following day. I was to receive an award and I had a flight to catch. I was in a rush, you could say, but I knew Karl was unwell, so I wanted to visit him before I left. To begin with it was nice, it was evident we had known each other a long time. We were like brothers, we could talk about anything. Of course, there was a little alcohol involved, but isn't alcohol always involved when close male friends spend time together? After a few hours the mood changed. Yes, it was a very clear switch: he hardened in some way and it didn't feel good.

And when I wanted to go, around three or four in the morning, he wouldn't let me. I have a plane to catch, I told him, I have to get to Kastrup. But he refused, he wouldn't let me out. It really felt like this went on for an eternity. Sometimes, when men spend time together, it can be hard to tell what's for real and what's a game. The banter can turn harsh, but most of the time nothing's meant by it, it's just people showing they're not to be messed with. Let me out, I said, trying to fill my voice with authority. No, said Karl. He locked the front door and put the key in his pocket. There was a long silence, I was standing in front of him, looking him in the eye. Unlike me, he possessed a natural authority. Had we been brothers, he would have been the big brother, even though I was older. You have no right, I ventured. Quiet, you're going to stay here with me and then I'm going to kill you and then my father and then myself. Only my son will be allowed to live. He said that and then he hit me hard across the face. I lost my balance and fell. He stood over me. I was lying on the ground, looking up at him. Something happened to his face and then he went into the kitchen and closed the door. I was shaken, incapable of thinking clearly, but after a while I at least managed to get up from the floor and sit on the sofa. I wondered whether I should jump out of the window, or at least open it and call for help, but it was as if I was paralysed. I was tired, couldn't come to a decision, and in the end I must have fallen asleep there on the sofa. I woke up to find Karl pulling my hair, lifting up my head and turning my face towards the window. It was morning. See that light? he said, pointing at the sky. Before it dies, you will. What? Die. Before it gets dark. I swear to you. Look, it's getting dark. You don't think I'm serious. Neither of us said anything for a very, very long time. Then I said: Stop it, Karl, you can't be serious. He replied, in a weak voice: I'm going to kill you before the sun goes down. You see the light out there? Before it dies, you will. Before the sun goes down, I swear. I closed my eyes.

*

My eyes are closed. It gets dark and then it gets light. This is happening now. I'm crying. He's laughing. We're as one, it feels like. We've become one, Karl and I. We're in my head, in my brain, somehow. We're shaking blood-stained hands. It's completely impossible to speak to him, he's unreachable. At first I think his eyes are inhuman, but as I think that, I think too that they are human, they are. Or like an animal's. Like at the zoo. Or in the forest or the sea or a park or out of this world, or like one time, when we were little, when we were taking care of a rabbit that had myxomatosis. But one time he comes home with closed-off eyes. One time there's a fire in the rubbish bin. One time we're sitting by a lake, fishing for carp. We fill a whole bucket. Karl has great big scabs on his knees. He shows me a Swiss army knife, made by Victorinox, and asks if I want to run away to Zurich with him. One time we go to Leipzig and Jena together. Now the leftovers are rotting in the kitchen sink. Neither of us can drink water. Neither of us takes out the rubbish. Karl picks up pieces of paper and books from the floor and reads aloud. He asks if I understand. I don't know what to say in response. And then I see that he's cut into one of his tattoos, it's the one with orchids and various kinds of spiders. I just took the knife, he says, and cut a notch by the stalk and stabbed the spiders in the eyes. You're bleeding! Come on, let's get you to the hospital, I say, hopefully. And a few scratches by the spiders' legs, or arms, or eyes, and a deeper cut up to the sun. He falls asleep in the green armchair, wakes up. *War ich nicht immer ein guter Junge*, he sings, *war ich nicht immer schön und nett?* He falls asleep on the sofa. He wakes up in bed. It gets dark and gets light. The fridge hums almost constantly. There's paper all over the floor, piling up, newspapers, books, promotional leaflets. If he spills wine on the floor he doesn't clean it up. He blames most things on me. Everything continues, never ends, feels like it's never going to end. I sit on the sofa for a long time, my elbows resting on my knees and my thumbs against my eyes, rubbing and pressing hard. Sometimes he sleeps constantly, sometimes just for a while, sometimes I do, for a while, sometimes we hug. Then he'll start flailing about. Saying dickhead, idiot, worthless. He says this is how we should spend our time, and I think if he was poor this could never happen, but he says he's glad his father is rich, he's so fucking rich, he says, out in fucking Vellinge. And you, he says, you're my little slave. Useful, in spite of everything. Let's go to Vellinge later, he says. And then I'll show you some really vile things. You want me to tell you? He clears his throat and it makes him sound like the old man he's become. Let me tell you I was born in a village outside of Bitterfeld, he says, it was the year of the revolution, 1917. No, wait, I mean, it was my father, my dad, who was born then. I was born later, when my father was in the Brownshirts. It was 1939, the year of the war. Then we came to Sweden, together, that was in the sixties, and now I'm here and Dad has crawled off into his cave in Vellinge. I say I know, that I know him. Ugh! he says, slapping me on the back of my head, you don't know anything, you'll never be able to understand me or my father, turn on the TV instead, the news is on now. He says I'll never understand anything. He says I'll see, later, in Vellinge. He screams and laughs, and paces back and forth across the creaking wooden floor, and he smokes and scratches himself on his spiders, by their eyes. Do you think my father has things from the Second World War? Do you think so? Daggers with swastikas and cutlery and things like that? You think so? You think my dad has soaps and drums and lampshades and whips, eh? You're bleeding! I say. Look, your boxers are all red and the boils on your face – he just sneers – you look like a monster, it's sick. Like an alien. Yeah. And the orchids are lovely and white, they glow so beautifully on your body, like angels almost, makes me think of that painting of cherubs, like snow, I think of our whole childhood, like white orchids on a body, cut to pieces, I think a load of thoughts, I think of the hills we rode sledges on, I think about how it felt exciting and safe at the same time, it never feels like that now, now most things are boring and threatening, I think about how they're called seraphim, I remember now, they sing beautifully, rock me to sleep where I lie, snugly wrapped, it's snowing outside the window but I'm warm and dry, and I think about freedom, but Karl just laughs at that, *Königstrasse*, he laughs scornfully, *der Weg zur Freiheit*, he laughs, just like we said in Bitterfeld, he says, but I still think about freedom, because that's what the cherubs and the seraphim sing about from their cotton-wool clouds, I jump between the white puffs and laugh, and I think about the future, my great future, that it's in my hands, like tiny little seeds planted in little rows in the little palms of my hands, and I'm not afraid of anything, because I know there are arms that can catch me, down there among the white flowers, if I were to fall, in the snow, among the spiders, and their soft webs, euphoria on Ferris wheels, white flowers with stars on them, protected species of animals in nature reserves, soft fur that smells of summer, workers in overalls reading books and holding bunches of colourful balloons, toffee apples and sweetly twisting peppermint rock. I think about the taste of rust and the smell of damp leather, the sound of valves and pistons and I think again and again about how it feels to rub your small, soft palms against large, rough ones marked by decades of shifts, I think of those tormented hands, punctured by needles, marred by untreated oedema, plagued by rheumatism, with nicotine-stained tips, scars on the knuckles, on the wrists, I think of shaking hands lifting spoons, and the child's hand running a finger along the lines of the adult palm, drumming on a callous, trying to straighten a stiff joint. Were these hands not also comforting and exciting, was it not also an adventure to hold one's childish hand against an adult body, against the hair, the angles, the slackness, to press one's nose into the strong scents, the moisture, was it not a premonition of the form things would take, with time, with work, with sickness and pleasure, or did all these sensations belong to the realm of the forbidden, is that why I'm thinking about them, are these in truth two versions of my own hand touching each other, is it my nose pressing into the sweat and the hair of my own armpit, now that it will soon be too late for everything, now Karl is standing before me, naked, over sixty-five years old, tattooed, deranged, revoltingly fat, ready to explode, abso-lutely ready to carry out these actions that neither of us can fathom, now that he's mocking every thought I have, now he's using his body to destroy mine, now he's creating these antitheses, this disarray. Is he not right when he says I know nothing about him, that I don't know him – after all, I don't even know myself, it was he who pointed that out, you don't even know yourself, so how can you determine what is right and not right? What you do is no more than a shadow of what you had hoped to do, and you will never find other truths than the fickle truths of your own experience. Is he really saying that, or is he reading from one of the books on the floor? He fills the whole room, I'm unable to think, he is forcing me out of myself, I don't know whether he's the one talking or if it's me, making him talk inside my head. Is this a hard man standing before me? I think about how soft his skin is. He says it smells of musk, I say vanilla. I say cherry and apricot, I say violet and mint-flavoured chewing gum, not musk, I say rose water and eucalyptus, jasmine and lemongrass, but he insists, repeats the word musk, occasionally adding the word ant. Look, he says, showing me his arms, legs, belly, can't you see that all this is clay, don't you see the ooze, don't you see the earth, the traces of roots and rotten leaves? Can't you see that this is a pithy, musty body I live in? Don't contradict me.

Yes. And I wake to find Karl burning me with a cigarette, then he roars so loud the neighbours start banging on the wall, or the floor or the wall or the ceiling or the floor or the wall or the floor and he tells me people die all the time, most of them are Americans, in cultural terms, because Americans took over the world in the fifties, but a man in a white hoodie passes the window and it says SWEDEN, he's talking on the phone and he looks cold. It's misty out there. I have a shave and recall that someone was here during the night. Some kind of dog was here, putting its nose in my face as I slept. When I ask Karl about it, he doesn't reply. Just says, Psycho. Psycho.

I'm not your therapist. He sits in the kitchen, fiddling with some electronic gizmo, a radio or a phone or something similar, and I lie down on the sofa. I think this is unbearable. The uncertainty, the arbitrariness. I pretend I'm a young man travelling for work. I have a salaried job and I pay tax and I'm part of an employment benefit fund. I'm in a hotel room. I turn on the TV, try to relax. I have a whisky, then another. It's a programme with doctors in green scrubs talking about illnesses and about ageing, and one of the doctors sits at a strange kind of desk, you can see his legs, his trousers are too short, like a nerd would wear, and he says: I'm a sledgehammer coming to crush death. After a few hours I stand up. My back is aching. I have no idea how long I've been here now. Long enough to construct some kind of normality, that much I know. A schema of what is permissible. What is possible. The apartment and its rooms. The mess on the floor. His body and his words. My body, my words. I open the window and look out over Kungsgatan, which has been called one of Malmö's most 'racially pure' streets – lined, moreover, with treasures of national romanticism. I don't know who said that, I know in any case that it wasn't Karl, I'm sure of that. I open the window but I don't escape. I don't jump. I can't. I lean out into the rain and see him walking along down there. *Suck nourishment*, he screams for all he's worth as he crosses the avenue. He's a ludicrous sight, anyone who didn't have to endure his blows would see that. He moves, bloodthirsty, noticeably intoxicated, suit and tie, an off-licence bag in his hand. I can see some teenagers laughing at him, from a safe distance, yes, they probably think he's some ridiculous old duffer from Germany. They don't even know what the GDR was. Suck nourishment, he repeats. Why would he say something like that? I imagine him picturing a mosquito. A gigantic green mosquito, an alien. What else can Karl see? This is what Karl can see, this is what Karl says: Someone is standing beneath me. I'm telling him to suck nourishment from the blood-stained spike sticking out of my abdomen. It's twisted like an intestine. Covered in mucus. My violence courses through everything. He's in my power. I stroke him if he's good. If he's good I tell him so. And I give him compliments. And medals I stole from my father. And food. Nourishment. As long as he's normal. As long as he's thinking the right thoughts. As long as he lies still. If I kill him he'll die a thousand deaths. When I touch him he changes. I hold his skull in my hands and press hard. I press him to my chest. I can feel the contours of his cranium. I know I could crush it. I can picture the bone-white structures. I could poke a finger in through one of the hollows. When I press he bends. Gives way. He's soft when I am hard. Silent when I speak. Small when I am large. I refrain from crushing him, and in return I want nothing but his gratitude. He means nothing to me; I mean everything to him. When he thinks, he thinks my name. Again and again, in different variations. I scream and take up all the space. This is me. It feels good. My body becomes focused when we speak. I enjoy just standing here watching. I enjoy watching him attentively. I like to have disorder around me and order inside me. Everything is heightened. I'm weak, but even in my weakness I am strong. That's how it is. Even when I lose, I am winning. I think about what will happen. About what I will do. I do the things I like doing, the things that get results. I don't think so much about intentions, only consequences. My common sense is choleric, my desire razor sharp, I can say anything at all.

Yes. And when Karl comes back I'm leant over the sink in the bathroom, washing my armpits. The door to the apartment slams into the bathroom door and he starts screaming again, though this time with a smile. He's carrying a load of shopping bags, they're full of clothes and tools and magazines and chocolate and other things. Presents, he calls them. He shows me his shopping list. It consists of a dozen or so items, all crossed off. Look, he says. I can do it all. I got my hands on every single fucking thing. You should never doubt me because then you'll be for it. Among other things, he gives me a yellow T-shirt with a green palm tree on it. He pinches me on the cheek. Puts some coffee on, undresses and sits down to take a shit with the door open. I lie down on the bed and pretend I have to sleep because I've got an important meeting the next morning. We are managers who need to make an important decision. I mustn't forget there's a new training schedule from Monday, that I have to call and book a table at the restaurant ahead of Saturday, buy some more vitamins and mouthwash, and drop off some shirts at the dry-cleaner's. And I have to pay the bills and get the oil changed and call a handyman who can stop the toilet running, it keeps me up at night, which in turn makes me perform poorly at work, it's unsustainable. Yes. But before I close my eyes I notice he has a tag around one ankle. Is that the only reason I'm here? To keep him company in his prison? The room starts spinning as I stand up and I panic, and for the first time ever it's me roaring, that's how it feels. But he sits calmly on his white chair, scratching his spiders and orchids and flames and crowns of thorns and letters written in Fraktur, and calls me a hysteric. Go and lie down you stupid cow, you hysteric, and it's then that I decide to murder him. I'm going to persecute and murder him, and skin his revolting body and grind his heart muscle to a pulp, if he even has one. I sit in front of the TV, I'm going to sentence him to death, but nothing happens and I nod off. Yes. And Karl wakes me, puts a chair against the wall and tells me how worthless I am. Yes, you're useless. But that doesn't go far enough, he says, you're not only worthless, that's putting it much too mildly, I think, it's much too neutral. The fact is you're unnecessary. As in, surplus. You see the difference? Your life is ballast. I don't know if he's right in what he says. Every time he pauses in his speech I think I should contradict him again. Get up and maybe even get angry and push him over. But it never happens. I don't reply. Instead I think about how time runs out in situations like this, how everything stands still and rushes away from you in every direction – all at the same time. Everything moves quickly, outside and inside of me. It's just me, the membrane between inside and outside, that remains still.

Yes. And Karl's son comes to visit, in a taxi, from the south of the city. I have to go out and pay for the journey, because the boy's only six or seven years old, his parents have forbidden him to touch money. I don't know what his name is and they don't tell me. Karl calls the boy 'Matey' and Matey says Dad in return. I don't want to say Matey so I say You and try to make eye contract. But it doesn't work, so in the end I say Matey too. While Matey is there, Karl doesn't hit me, doesn't shout, he just smokes in the kitchen, under the fan. Think of Matey's lungs, he says. And I try to picture his lungs in cross-section. They are piggy-pink inside. Matey's wearing a tiger suit. Tail and all. I've put on my new T-shirt and am making him some porridge. When Karl's face starts bubbling, he goes into the toilet and locks the door. Me and Matey sit at the kitchen table and eat porridge. I ask Matey if he likes watching TV, I tell him about the sledgehammer that's coming to crush death and he tells me he's a tigerman. Your dad is kind most of the time, I say, but he can be cruel too. You don't know what desire is yet, but your dad's desire is razor sharp. Matey vomits up a mouthful of porridge in response. When his dad comes back he has a large bandage wrapped around his face and I can hardly stop laughing. He tells Matey it's bedtime now. Go and brush your teeth and take off your suit. And when Matey isn't listening, he whispers in my ear that he's going to kill me if I touch his son. You look like a mummy, I laugh. I can't take you seriously when you look so ridiculous. I don't feel afraid when Matey's here. Can you tell me a story about cowboys? Matey is lying in bed, the tiger suit stretched out next to him. Karl tells a story about a group of farmers who try to fix a combine harvester without success. Matey toys with the suit and says the story is rubbish. But his dad doesn't take the criticism to heart, he just carries on in a gruff voice. I fall asleep.

*

Yes. And when Matey has gone back home to his mum, Karl beats me and when I wake up I'm ashamed of how imprudent I was. He yells at me. I'm trying to reason with you but it seems to be impossible. Be quiet, go and sit over there and be quiet. Listen to me, he says. I turn on the TV in the middle of his booming speech. This is not a prison, he says. This is no Guantánamo or Hohenschönhausen, if that's what you were thinking. I'm no ayatollah or pope or dictator. I haven't said you have to say *sieg heil* every time I come into the room or that you have to sing my national anthem. Look at my hands. Do they look like weapons? No one's forcing you to do anything. You're free, you just need to realise that yourself. You have to want it, really yearn for it deep down, fight for it. Battle, battle, battle! That's the only thing that matters. And in order to battle you need an enemy. Look at me. Look at me, Karl says. I look at him, as I turn up the sound on the TV and try to look relaxed. What do I have to say to make you understand? Do I have to explain it all from the beginning? He gets on his knees and starts rummaging through the papers on the floor. An advert comes on the TV. He tells me to turn off the noise and gets up with a book in his hand. Look here, he says, and I turn off the TV. He flicks through the book. You're disturbed. I'm not using the term 'mentally ill' here, because mental illness is intermittent, while someone who's disturbed experiences feelings and stimuli constantly. Someone who is depressed doesn't necessarily spend every month of their lives going round feeling depressed, but someone who has a personality disorder is disturbed on a day-to-day basis. Always. Karl looks up from the book to see if I'm listening. I don't know if he's reading from the book or making it all up. I don't know if it matters. This disturbance must have expressed itself in childhood and be detrimental to everyday life. And yeah, I guess I can say that your state of mind is highly detrimental to your everyday life, because who wants to go around being unhappy, spiteful and overflowing with ideas of a dubious nature, when they could do something altogether different instead? Who wants to spend their time spreading lies they actually believe? I know what you're thinking now, Karl says. He sits down and exhales. Then he goes on, calmly and collectedly. There are areas of obscurity, I'm aware of that. Areas of unclarity that render the analysis more difficult. That's due to the fact that personality disorders can be divided into different categories, with different behaviours associated with them. In its handbook *Diagnostic and Statistical Manual of Mental Disorders*, also known as DSM-IV, the American Psychiatric Association, or APA for short, classifies various personality disorders. One example looks like this: Cluster A – odd or eccentric disorders: Paranoid, Schizoid, Schizotypal. Cluster B – dramatic, emotional or erratic disorders: Antisocial, Borderline, Histrionic, Narcissistic. Cluster C – anxious, fearful disorders: Avoidant, Dependent, Obsessive-compulsive. I know what you're thinking now. Paranoid, histrionic and obsessive-compulsive. What's the problem? I'll explain. You think you're normal but you're not. You say this is 'normal' and that's 'abnormal', but how can you know that? If we were to use you as a basis, I mean, what you do when you are you, how you look when you're wearing your clothes, how it feels inside your body, in your brain, when you dress up as a man, in boxers, a suit and tie, and a rapier, and it's clear you think that this is me, when you bleed, when you think, when you sleep, only then can all this be normal. Is this what you mean? Karl says, dejectedly. Is this what you maintain? Do you think there are two kinds of people? A, B? Or more? A, B, C, D? Cluster Alpha, blah, blah, blah, Cluster Omega?

Yes. I don't know. The only thing I want is to be alone with you for a short while, to rip everything to shreds and feed it to the animals – and you can't even give me that?

Yes. And a few hours later we're lying beside one another on the sofa. Our pride, says Karl, is something we must never lose. Without it we're nothing. You see how people look at me, you've seen that, right?

You are alone all your life, that's how it is, there's no other truth. And if you don't have your pride, you can't protect yourself against them. We're holding one another. I ask if he misses Matey, but he refuses to answer. Just hold me, he whispers. I realise he was right all this time. He really does smell of musk, not vanilla. The worst thing, he says, is being buried in the desert sand, all the way to your chin, and being left to die under the hot sun. Believe me. Or being skinned alive. The worst thing, he says, is that my power doesn't reach beyond the walls of this house. Home, it's everything. Sorry if I hurt you. I'm going to take care of you from now on, I'll bathe you and put food on the table. I'll be like a father to you, and like a friend at the same time. Take care of you. Hum lullabies and rub your lumbar spine, your shoulder blades, your back. I see you need it, that you're sensitive and fragile. If we go out together I'll do the best I can to protect you. I promise I'll do my best to be strong and resourceful, muscular and attentive.

Yes. And with that promise ringing within me I fell asleep, and before I woke Karl got up and fetched the hammer, which he used to beat in my head. There was mess everywhere. And the darkness came, and the light came, a few times, yes, it took a few days before it was all brought to light. The disfigured one lay where he lay. Now and then I would look out over Kungsgatan to see if anyone was on their way. I looked out over the avenue, the gravel path, the café tables, the cyclists riding by. His car was still there, he'd missed his plane but everything else remained. The fire engines were dispatched, the neighbours walked their dogs, they walked by with buggies, they talked to each other, they went to work in the morning and came home in the evening. Everything was just as usual. They even greeted me, looked up at the window where I stood, and they waved, as though they knew me, as though they were familiar with my struggle, as though they knew what my name was. Yes, it was as though they really cared about me. And I, with a feeling of strength and unity, waved back every time.

ON THE WAVES

I turn on the radio and hear a man talking about his cock.

Yes, as I listen, I must surmise – once again (or at least, that's how it feels, since even though it's impossible to say for sure when or how (or indeed, *whether*) I've experienced this before, I still recognise something in the situation as such, that is, as a *situation*, a circumstance, state, position), once again I find myself in a scenario involving two people, one of whom is *well situated*, and the other, you might say, is *ill situated* – this is how life is here: the voice of a man, talking about his cock on the radio. Though he doesn't call it a cock, he says *penis*, and describes it, using three or four adjectives.

I look out the window and see a plumber. I don't know him, not really, but I did once play Texas hold 'em with him, and I know his name is Raúl Schulze. He stands there, talking on the phone as he paces the pavement back and forth.

Ewa and Dragica, my neighbours – my flabby old neighbours, gossiping their way through early retirement – are sitting on Dragica's balcony, smoking and drinking coffee. They're the ones who call themselves that, it's not just an (unwarranted) thought of mine. ('Magda,' they say, 'won't you come and sit with us? We've got so much in common, flabby old women gossiping our way through early retirement. Grab a bottle of vino and come over.' Speak for yourselves, I think.)

Dragica has a little dog that licks her face. She lets him do it, even though it gives her a rash. Or maybe it just makes the rash she already has worse, in any case it looks awful, like she's been washing her face with grit or sand.

Ewa only has one breast – it's obvious, even though she tries to hide it with toilet paper or bags of peas or whatever. Her son has a harelip and got done for manslaughter. Ewa says that when he killed that man he'd been grossly insulted and provoked, but I've heard, from people who were there, that it was the son (his name began with D-something: Denno, Danny, Dennis, maybe even Dante – which would be kind of funny, I guess – but I can't remember exactly) who was harassing a group of people for several hours, and that someone got sick of it and smacked him one (gave him a *walloping*, as my brother and I used to say to each other: *You want a walloping, or what?*) and after that he completely flipped out, slashing about wildly with a Mora knife. But I don't know what to believe. How would I? On the one hand, people say all kinds of things about each other, they lie and they slander, they have their favourites and their grudges. On the other hand, you get the sense sometimes that rumours and gossip are mostly based on something, that the old cliché *no smoke without fire* really is true.

My penis, the man says again, egged on by an overly enthusiastic, giggly woman's voice. It seems he's a poet. I'd been hoping for the news, something interesting, something productive, something about climate change or at least the weather, so I can prepare for tomorrow's trip to Ystad, where my son (whose weariness and general perplexity at life are increasingly resembling my own) has been living for the last three years with a woman he insists on calling *my old lady* – but instead I got a dose of oral cock inserted into my ear. It makes me so depressed that instead of turning the dial to another station I turn the radio off. This leads to an almost unpleasant silence.

But soon the sounds force their way in. I hear the workings of the fridge, distant traffic, the hoarse chit-chat of Ewa and Dragica, birds.

I think there's probably something wrong with my life. But what? I think there are various ways of describing the issue, the problem.

Right now, today, I think it's probably to do with the fact I've lost my curiosity. I think it's as simple as that. I can't be bothered with anything any more. I used to be interested in the world. Once upon a time I even thought that I myself was an interesting part of it. Gradually I woke up from this embarrassing delusion, but even then I was still interested in the rest of the world, in everything else that's in it, everything that moves, everything that grows, communicates, cultivates and is cultivated. The whole business.

I don't know where I got it from, this interest. I was the first in my family to finish university. Or the only one, I should say. My parents weren't interested in anything, not even themselves. They just lived, survived, until one day they didn't any more. Dad had a heart attack in the toilet of the local pub, and Mum got stomach cancer and faded away in a damp-ravaged hospital room that stank of bleach. My friends only cared about alcohol, sex, money and television. Most of them had to be content with the latter, in spades. From early morning until late at night. Each programme more moronic than the last. I'm still the only person in my social circle and my home to have finished university. Now it makes no difference, because I neither can, nor want to, work with anything at all, but it used to. Not that I was particularly intelligent or successful. But I was there. I sat through the lectures and seminars, and I read the books and took part in the discussions, and I didn't feel stupid, I kept up, and I understood – maybe not everything, but most of it. I didn't make a fool of myself. I wasn't pretending when I sat at those seminar tables, reflecting on multi-faceted abstractions, analysing complex patterns and asking difficult questions. It was real, I was the one thinking those things, I was the one feeling things in response to statements and theories and analyses which had as good as zero bearing (yes, maybe less than zero (if that's possible) considering their parasitic nature) on the world beyond the university and the application forms of the Science Council.

What happened then? What was it that made me lose interest? Yes. You tell me. I don't know. It was probably a combination of factors. Not least the instinct that behind all these clever words lay nothing but simple impulses. Behind all these words on liberation and emancipation and radicalism and knowledge and resistance and freedom and possibility and science and rationality and reciprocity (yes, in my Master's thesis I discussed the concept of the reciprocity principle in the late modern philosophy of law in relation to the so-called *golden rule*: 'Do unto others as you would have them do unto you'), and even love and holiness – behind all these words was nothing but a self-involved desire to advance one's career. The critique of the system was no more than a way (admittedly an advanced one) to progress one's own position in the system. The radical gestures were a way of further entrenching the status quo.

I had a friend who vanished into the world of US academia. After four months came a letter that contained a sentence I still remember:

Left-wing academia as a cocktail party, the lives and fates of workers, migrants and the poor serving primarily – if not exclusively – to make up the durable fabric from which a career is woven.

And then, on top of it all, this poet's cock.

I wonder if he's still talking about it. I hear a sound I think is probably coming from a reversing lorry. I run the palm of my hand over the oilcloth. Little grains stick to the sweat. Salt? Or sugar? I lick my hand. Salt. I remember Raúl telling me he was in the process of saving money for a big trip, that he was talking about 'the Venezuelan tragedy' and (rightly) mocking the other card players because they knew nothing about Latin America, I mean really nothing, they didn't even know which was bigger, Brazil or Ecuador. I remember I lost 300 kronor, and afterwards Raúl bought me two cans of beer in some kind of futile attempt at cheering me up.

I can't hear the voices on the radio, but the waves go right through my head. Right through my skin. The radio waves and their poet's cock force their way through everything.

I rub the palm of my hand on the top of my thigh, mere inches from my own genitals.

Raúl gets into a van bearing the words *Heart Drainage Services* and drives off. Guess it's time for his nine o'clock break. His genitals rest in his underwear.

Hugo Chávez is dead. Soon Maduro will die too.

Dragica and Ewa laugh at something. Their genitals are hidden behind the metal of the balcony, as is their underwear.

Thank God humans are relatively civilised animals, in spite of everything, I think, sniffing my fingers. An artificial lavender scent and something indistinct beneath it. Perhaps the scent of my own sweat, which I can't smell because I'm so accustomed to it.

Thank God, I think then, that we can't see radio waves.

TRAJECTORIES

This might not really have anything to do with my life, but I can't stop thinking about the story of the fifty-six-year-old man, who worked for Sweden's national security service and was convicted of gun crime and possession of narcotics. Once a central, reliable cog in the intelligence service, now disowned and dismissed. He loses his job of course, and his wife – a successful corporate lawyer whose father is some big local businessman – divorces him. When he's served his prison sentence, he moves to a flat in one of the three-storey municipal apartment blocks on the outskirts of a small town in southern Sweden. He starts smoking cigarettes and often sits on his fully glazed balcony, from where he has a good view out across a large patch of wasteland and a field. He sits there watching the sun rise, if it's morning, or, if it's evening, the young guys dealing drugs in the bike sheds of the neighbouring building. He gets a new job as a so-called 'hospitality facilitator' at a nightclub. One morning he comes home from a shift and sits on the balcony with a cup of tea. He watches the sun rise over the field and the wasteland.

The shotters are still asleep, he thinks, his words free of irony. He dwells on an image: a young man, sleeping in the bed his mother makes for him each day. His breathing, his sheets, his open mouth, his dry lips and the saliva making his teeth glisten. The duvet, bunched up in the corner of the bed; the design printed on it is of three tiger cubs.

He sees people hurrying to work, children going to school, parents walking along pushing buggies. All this is an answer to something, he thinks. But what?

He goes down to the street and over to the bus stop. When the bus comes he gets on. He travels into the town centre. Wanders at random. Along the high street and back, parallel and perpendicular streets. It's foggy. He thinks about his father. How disappointed he would be if he were alive to see this. It feels like something terrible is going to happen, he thinks. On one level I should take my own life, it would make sense. But I'm not going to.

He stands in the town square, under the statue – Pierre Hubert L'Archevêque's statue of Queen Christina, after Sébastien Bourdon's 1653 painting, *Christina of Sweden on Horseback* – and looks up at the queen, her whip pointing up at the clouds, the rearing horse, the peregrine falcon perched at the base of the horse's tail, and he thinks: that is a statue that exudes life and power, control over the chaos of possibility, and well, he doesn't want to think virility, but he thinks virility. It reminds him of his youth and he realises his life will never be like that again. He lowers his eyes, rubs them and thinks: here I stand. Surrounded by people. They're everywhere, but there are no ties between us. They are speaking, using words, but I can't hear them. Or, I can hear them, but I don't understand what they're saying. Or, I do understand, but I can't take it in. Can't make sense of it. Every approach also repels. I'm so boundlessly lonely and it renders me completely dependent on everyone around me. Everything disappears for me because I have it inside me. No one is anywhere, nothing exists, still something aches. Connections, openings.

There's a sound.

My father would never say he cried, but rather: *My eyes filled with tears.* But I never saw them. I saw nothing. And that's how it is still: I see nothing.

He thinks it's time to go home and get some sleep. He crosses the square and as he does he imagines his mother rubbing a sticky salve over his eyelids. The salve is made of honey and smells sweet and heavy.

He hears a child's voice, it's his own: *We have six beehives outside the kitchen, Mother and Father look after them.*

He sees his father, hears him say: *But it's not all that much work.* His father's voice is deep and resonant with warmth. He takes a sip of coffee from the white cup with narrow green stripes. He chuckles. He doesn't sound old, but still there's something old-fashioned about his chuckle, as though his voice had been recorded fifty years ago, a hundred years ago, or in the seventeenth century, during Queen Christina's time. He chuckles the way people used to chuckle, says, *The bees do most of the work*, and puts his cup down on the saucer, which is also white with thin green stripes. *They're efficient little creatures. Like projectiles, they are. In contrast to certain people. Yeah, just think, there are people who are less efficient than a bee. They're satellites. Constantly bound to another body, constantly bound to another object.*

Projectiles or satellites, he thinks.

Is it a question that needs an answer? Or does it simply hide another, much more important question?

THE READING
THIEF

Only a few minutes into the conversation I realise it's over. We'll never come together, me and him. There's no space for it, no common ground, no common language, nothing in common at all. Nothing, aside from the fact we've both been given our roles in this drama, in this predictable make-believe in which each of us is our own protagonist, each the other's nemesis.

Or perhaps we do have a common language, but we use it in completely different ways, for different reasons and with different goals? Unfortunately it falls to me to provide the answer, for the time being. But there's something. Something hard, impenetrable between us. Something that makes it impossible for us to come together, even if we wanted to.

No justice, no peace, perhaps. At whose cost?

His face, his eyes, his whole body and its motions, all that I was completely oblivious to just a few hours ago suddenly sparks a hot contempt in me. A desire, a furious desire. It happened surprisingly quickly. We said hello, exchanged a few looks, uttered a few phrases and assumed our previously assigned positions.

Somewhat simplified: there was a room, a table, two chairs.

No. It's not a conversation. Not really. You couldn't say that. It's an interrogation. That much is clear. He asks his questions, I look him in the eye and consider the question, or pretend to consider it and say something. Not necessarily an answer. Sometimes it's a counter-question, or an *I don't know*. At first I considered trying the *no comment* strategy, but in this case I think it would be to my disadvantage since it's a strategy that in some way implies an admission. And that's not where I'm at, not yet.

Our roles are very clear. Legality versus legitimacy. It's an ancient scene playing out here, that much I know. I'm thinking of Socrates, though I realise the comparison is a lame one. No, I really don't mean to tease, and yet there's something, something . . .

What's he thinking about? What does he know? Can he sense the ancient essence that lies behind our words and gestures? Hardly. He knows nothing but the paper in front of him. And the walls, the floor, the ceiling. The table, the chairs, the door. An apparently eternal present.

And then the absent element that is the actual motor here, the main ingredient.

The thing that has disappeared.

'You were the last person to leave the establishment.'

Pause.

'Do you have any explanation?'

After this last word, he leans his head back a little and I can see right into his nostrils. Two – from this angle, rather peculiar – holes in his head.

'No,' I say.

When he doesn't respond to my answer, I add:

'I don't know. What is it that's disappeared? I don't know. I didn't take anything.'

He seems happy with my answer, strangely enough. He gives a wan smile and nods.

'You were the only person cleaning the establishment on the night in question.'

He speaks his sentences one at a time, with a short pause between each one.

'You were the only person in the main office on the night in question.'

Pause.

'The only one.'

Pause.

'Do you understand the implications of that?'

I sit in silence for a while, let the time pass, am careful to meet his gaze. Then I spread my hands. A small, controlled gesture.

'Well, I'm not sure what to say.'

He looks at the papers in front of him, straightens them.

'The thing that disappeared, if, indeed, you don't know what it is, was something . . .'

Now he's even pausing mid-sentence.

'. . . valuable, something . . .'

'. . . how should I put it . . .'

'. . . covetable.'

Pause.

'But I think you know that?'

'OK,' I say. 'No, I actually don't know what it was that went missing. I have no idea.'

'You were the last one out.'

Pause.

'There's no other explanation.'

Pause.

'At least, not a feasible one.'

Pause.

'Not an admisstable one.'

I note his misstep. Is he that uncertain? He was about to say 'acceptable', but it sounded too simple, so he tried to replace it with the more mannered, *judicial*-sounding 'admissible'. The result was a crippled mish-mash that means something else entirely. Nonsense. He is trying to exude power and authority but achieves the opposite.

'Plus . . .'

'. . . all the other indicators.'

'You understand that, right?'

'The risk factors.'

'And it's hardly as if there's no motive.'

'Considering your salary, I mean.'

He mumbles these last words, almost to himself. Is it a provocation?

'So . . .'

'. . . what do you say?'

'I don't know,' I reply.

'No . . .'

'I don't know,' I repeat.

'. . . OK.'

'But now circumstances are speaking . . .'

'. . . for themselves . . .'

'The circumstances are speaking clearly, against you, isn't that true.'

'But perhaps there are things you don't know,' I say.

'What might they be?'

'I don't know.'

'No, I don't think so.'

Pause.

'Do you?' he says.

He's starting to look a little irritated.

'Well, you seem to be a pretty smart guy.'

Pause.

'Do you think all this seems feasible?'

'I don't know. I'm just saying that you can't know everything. And you can't prove anything.'

Now he's grinning scornfully.

'You think we need to?'

How long have we been sitting here? I can feel my back aching. I'm starting to get thirsty. He's had a few sips from a plastic water bottle in his briefcase. His Adam's apple moved up and down as he drank and I saw how he ran his tongue over his front teeth after swallowing. And then came a quiet smacking noise and a soft sigh.

I look at him and try to concentrate on my own thoughts, my own images and fantasies. All to shut out the sound of his voice, his words, his questions. I know that every word he utters belongs to this room, to this moment. To the present, which I don't want to acknowledge.

It's hard, this stuff.

I close my eyes. Try to picture his face. I open my eyes again and look at him. He looks indifferent. He is talking. Everything he says ends in a question mark. Everything he says is shot through with threat and blame. Even the pauses, the silence. How can I answer?

I'm going to try and leave my body. I'm going to imagine a way out. I'll divide the room into two parts. Right and left. The line between them runs from an imagined point between his eyes. I think to myself that one side is black and the other is white. His body is grey, or black and white, like the television sets of my childhood when someone pulled out the antenna, a swarm of moving white and black specks.

Like, chaos. Tabula rasa.

It's impossible. I have to find the truth.

What am I doing here? How did I end up here?

It doesn't matter. I don't give a fuck, never had one to give. Or: *I don't work for nothing. Nothing came first, I'm used to bluffing.* Or whatever it was I was listening to when I got to work today and they said: Good morning, excuse me, can you come with me for a moment, and took me to the guy with the folder and the questions.

The whole scene reminded me of another time they hauled me in. That time I was walking along in the park behind the casino when they pushed me to the ground, sat on me, pulled my arms back, hard, a knee in my back, a hand over my mouth, and that provocative pressure over my nostrils so I couldn't breathe – open for a moment, then closed again, open for a moment, then closed again. I remembered the feeling of suffocation, the panic, but also, through it all, the thought that something else was waiting for me on the other side. Something good.

One day I'll look back on what's happening now and it will no longer be painful.

It will be a memory.

It will be images.

Echoes of images, reflections.

No sensory impressions.

Future.

There is a future.

And it's the same now. At some point in the future this room and this man will be memories. The chair, the table, the questions, and the pauses. The image of his face, the holes in his head. The threats and contempt. Nothing but memories, that grow fainter and fainter, more and more diffuse, with every day that passes, only to finally disappear completely. But I will still be here. The only one here.

Right?

No. Suddenly I realise I'm speaking to someone. Someone standing alongside me. I feel it. I know it. I start thinking about the unknown, hidden enemy in Anna Kavan, though the other way around – a friend. I realise that somewhere in the world, I have a loving friend, a sweetheart.

I don't know your name and I don't know what you look like. But I do know you're there and that I'm addressing you now. I can feel that you can hear me, that you're waiting for me. I can feel that you understand me. That you can support me. As I am. All of me.

So perhaps my words do count for something. Perhaps I can say something. Not everything, but something. Only idiots like him believe you can tell all. You already know that. That you can be exhaustive when it comes to these things. Or you can be consistent, without contradicting yourself. Honest. Direct. Calm. Free.

You know. That's not how it is. Nothing is. Nothing. We're left with our anxiety, in splinters of light. We're quiet, sluggish animals. Our bodies contend with decades and centuries of injustice, stored in our neural pathways.

But still.

Is there something? Something small? A seed? Or a husk?
A crushed one?

OK, I admit it. I'm a thief. Even as a child I was a skilled thief. So skilled that for several years, let's say when I was ten, eleven, twelve, thirteen, I considered – even dreamed of – a future career in theft.

It just happened. It just turned out that way. It felt natural, somehow. I would see something, want that thing, and then take that thing. It was that simple. I was soon a master shoplifter. Sweets, food, comics. There were few things I couldn't lift in a regular shop. I soon became quick and sharp-eyed with break-ins too. In flats and storage basements as well as warehouses and workplaces. With cars, motorbikes, mopeds I guess I was only moderately skilled, since I hadn't yet learned the art of hot-wiring, and because my body was still a little too small to manoeuvre the heavy vehicles. Bikes, on the other hand, those I've had my fair share of. And I've nicked a small mountain of coats, jackets, backpacks, handbags.

I even developed a talent for stealing from my own mother. Here, my thefts involved very small sums of money, a coin here or there, since she so rarely had any cash. 'It's so hard to make our benefits last the month,' she used to say. Which gave me a bad conscience, of course. A little, in any case. To compensate, I stole jewellery, toiletries and various ornaments to give to her. Rings, earrings, brooches. Small pictures and statuettes. Stones with magical powers: amethyst, rose quartz, malachite. Perfume and makeup. Or small, practical things for the house. Tin openers, knives, crystal ashtrays.

I stole at school of course. I took everything you could conceivably sell or trade for something else. Pens and other stationery. Cables, batteries, light bulbs. I stole from bookshops, libraries, record shops. Sometimes I even stole in church, mostly for the fun of it. Candles, rosaries, small icons. And I often nicked things when I was at friends' houses. Marbles, Lego, various kinds of trading cards.

My talents made me popular and respected in certain circles. And together with a couple of friends I planned and executed a large number of thefts and break-ins.

Apart from the thing with my mother I rarely suffered from a guilty conscience. In some ways I was just addressing a disparity. I couldn't understand why other people should be allowed to have things, lots of things, nice things, while I had nothing. And if I had something, it was most often bad. Our apartment was ugly. The furniture was tatty. All the *honest* toys were boring. My socks and underpants had holes in them, our towels were rough. The TV flickered so much you had to bang it hard regularly, the stereo crackled so much you could barely hear the music. Our cornflakes tasted of, like, petrol, and came in drearily designed packaging, the fish fingers were more flour than fish. My designer clothes were cheap copies that looked weird and often came apart at the seams. My haircut was a DIY catastrophe because my aunt overestimated her skill with trimmer fades. I didn't even have a bed, just a heap of foam chunks wrapped in fabric that we called a *sofa bed*, as if that made it any better.

But it never felt all that good, regardless of how much I got my hands on, gathered around me. Because even when I had money or nice things, good things, things that worked, I always knew they were worse than they actually were. After all, they were stolen. It was like I'd degraded them, dirtied them by association.

So even though I didn't go round feeling guilty, or let it get to me to the extent I changed my behaviour, I was conscious that what I was doing was, on a fundamental level, wrong. The seventh commandment and all that. Yeah, I was under no illusions. I revered neither the crime nor the punishment, I didn't turn my thefts into fetishes, like some miniature version of Jean Genet. I was a sinner. And because I was, in my own way, a child of faith, I would go to confession (though I kept to myself the bit about stealing from the church) and immediately everything would feel much, or at least a little, better again. I'd spent enough time on the pews to be able to quote what Jesus and the apostles said about judging others. I'll let God do the reckoning. No one else. That was what I thought.

When I say I was 'skilled', mostly I mean I had a talent for finding the right moment, weighing risk against profit, that I was fast and efficient, and, in some ways, invisible – but also, of course, that I never got caught. A basic principle, you could say.

Esse, non videri.

To be, not to seem to be – a motto I shared with the most successful and wealthy members of society, thieves and non-thieves alike. And for several years I stole without once getting caught. I was invincible. And then, well, I guess it was just a question of time.

I got lazy, it was mildly humiliating. An assistant in a music shop caught me red-handed as I pocketed a tuner. I managed to run out onto the street but they got me after 100 metres or so. The assistant grabbed me firmly by the scruff of the neck and dragged me back to the shop. Shame washed over me. It was a new kind of shame, and it was particularly embarrassing since I was carrying a bouquet of flowers at the time, I think they were tulips, which my mum had asked me to buy from the market that day because we'd been invited to a christening. It could have ended there, with me giving back the tuner and apologising, but it just so happened that a police car was patrolling. The assistant waved them over, explained the situation. The cops, who in some strange way managed to seem at once apathetic and eager, stood me against their car, spread my legs, and frisked me slowly and thoroughly on the busy street. Out of the corner of my eye I could see one of my classmates' parents watching. I wondered what they were thinking, feeling. Disappointment? Surprise? Contempt? Or did they think that everything was as it should be? Everything is as it is, after all. What it has become. I guess deep down we all know that.

To an outsider, it would seem like no big deal. I was a minor and it was a small, innocuous crime. But when the cops dragged me home my mum burst into tears, pretty theatrically (as I said, we know deep down), and after a while social services got involved. We had to go to meetings where I assured everyone present that this was the first time I'd stolen anything and that I would never, ever do it again (I was a skilled liar too, but that's another story (and a fact that should not be allowed to undermine your conviction that everything I am saying now is completely true)).

In time I really did stop thieving. But it took a couple of years, and even long after I'd stopped stealing on a daily basis, or a regular one, I would have relapses. Not least when I drank. Fancy wines and bottles of spirits would vanish from behind the bar. At house parties I always seemed to find something I thought I needed or wanted. Jewellery, cameras, CDs, perfumes, whatever, you get the gist.

The last time I stole I took a guy's phone in a restaurant. I just swept it into my pocket when he turned his back and then went grinning out into the cold winter night, where I quickly turned it off. But I didn't get far before I was struck by a regret I'd never felt before. I'd never felt this way in the process of the actual theft, in the heat of the moment, so to speak, and definitely not when I'd been drinking. But now this rueful feeling grew with every moment and I no longer wanted the phone. I turned and went back to the restaurant. The guy was going around searching for his phone, looking under chairs and tables, turning his jacket and backpack inside out. I went into the toilet and put it down next to the soap dispenser. Then I left, feeling noticeably lighter.

Now I was not only a thief but something more: a regretful robber, the penitent thief. I was the kin of Dismas, I learned from a book I read some years later, and Dismas is a saint, though the church never canonised him. It's he who, together with Gestas, is nailed up next to Jesus and hears the words: 'Amen, I say to you, today you will be with me in Paradise.'

It was liberating. Not only was I now under the protection of Saint Nicholas (Nicholas, also known as Santa Claus, is the patron saint of falsely accused persons, penitent thieves and prostitutes, among others), I could put my time into something that couldn't be stolen. The desire for things was gone, and I could focus on books and the library. On borrowing and returning. The cliché was true: knowledge really was a gift, a blessing. And as Dizzy Gillespie is said to have said: 'You can't steal a gift.'

So, I'd given up thieving, and believed I was no longer a thief. But it soon became apparent that I still identified as one. This became clear one day as I was listening to the radio and a programme came on about two journalists who'd been imprisoned under horrific conditions. They said they'd been treated 'like common thieves'. When I heard this I noticed myself feeling offended. Did we thieves – common or not, penitent or not – deserve such treatment? Was it right to punish us, humiliate us, even torture us? I couldn't let it go. And it seemed everyone around me (I no longer hung out with thieves) thought it was fair. My new friends spoke with contempt about people who stole, and they didn't distinguish between the propensity of the rich or the poor to steal. Everywhere there were warnings to beware of thieves. On signs, stickers and in wise words spoken between friends. I read something online about a city on the Med where the bookshops left books out at night. They were never stolen, you see, because 'readers don't steal, thieves don't read'. Which also, time after time, seems to be supported by riots and looting all over the world – where bookshops, for the most part, are left untouched. But perhaps this can be interpreted in another way.

I thought of all the books I'd stolen, from the library as well as from bookshops. I recalled Maja Ekelöf's 'I stole this paper, the pen too', and Abbie Hoffman's *Steal This Book*, which I once nicked three copies of from a 'radical' bookshop in Copenhagen, and I thought about Black Thoughts' *'It's crazy when you too real to be free / If you don't got no paper then steal this CD'*, and T. S. Eliot's 'Immature poets imitate; mature poets steal', and Joanna Demers' *Steal This Music*. And so on. I remembered reading about Roberto Bolaño's great hunger for reading, that it could match Borges's, but that the former, in contrast to the latter, stole most of his books. And I remembered my pride when I stole an anthology on nineteenth-century political ideas from the school library and then, lying on my 'sofa bed' in my room, read the section about Proudhon and his *What Is Property?* And the irritation I felt reading Harry Houdini's nasty book of snitchery *The Right Way to Do Wrong: An Exposé of Successful Criminals.*

Thou shalt not steal, sure. But the question was: who is the rightful owner? Isn't all wealth stolen anyway? And wasn't Christ himself supposed to come like a thief in the night?

I know. I know that shouldn't be taken literally. All I'm trying to say is that sometimes the thing that appears just is really unjust, and vice versa. And it might seem self-evident, but it's very hard to turn these insights into actions or practical stances. It leaves you feeling ambivalent, lonely.

That's why, for many years I've carried a quote with me wherever I go, since it's the first thing I write in every new notebook – which I have of course, in my new life, paid for. It's a quote by Clarice Lispector which, I think in my more sentimental moments, I have tattooed on my heart:

'If you've never stolen anything you won't understand me.'

The interrogator sitting in front of me, has he ever stolen anything? No, he can't have. Most probably he's committed worse crimes, various physical and psychological assaults, but a thief he is not. Even if I wanted to, see, it would be impossible to stand on an equal footing with the person who's sitting in front of me, asking his questions. This is the reason. It has nothing to do with language, its sources and purposes. He will never understand me. There's no common ground, nowhere to meet in the middle, because he's never stolen anything. He'll never understand, or even see, that my guilt contains my innocence.

But you, my darling, you are a thief like me, I'm convinced of that, though I don't yet know you. I know you are a regretful, penitent thief, who acts without seeming to be. I know that you hear me, that you see me, and I know you understand me and you wait for me. I'll come out to you soon.

Very soon.

NOTIONS

I keep little pieces of paper with quotes on them. Some I've found, others I wrote myself.

In some cases suicide is indefensible: it's simply disrespectful to those who are truly oppressed.

And: *There's one photo of him I keep. He's sitting on a park bench, his arms on the back. He's smiling. I've never seen another smile like that in my life.*

And: *Suicide represents what I'd call a privileged moment in the life of an individual.*

And: *The exploded and sewn-together heads of the children.*

And: *Le temps détruit tout.*

And: *I've never said you should commit suicide, I've just said that the mere thought of it can help us get through life. The thought that it is within our power to bring an end to our existence, that we can commit suicide at any time, if we want, holds an immense solace.*

And: *Become apotheosis.*

Right next to the hut where L lives, the children gather in a gravel yard. The hut has a plywood floor, four walls made of silver-grey metal sheeting with patches of cobalt paint, and a roof consisting of plastic sheets and tarpaulins. L says a few months ago, before their teacher left, it was a kind of makeshift school. Now the children meet here sometimes, to rest or to remember, I don't know. They sit and talk, throw stones, sing songs and play hopscotch. When

I walk past they tug at my clothes, begging for food and money. I tell them I don't have anything but they carry on for a while, then they give up and ask to play instead. I go inside, get a few of L's books with their big colour pictures. We sit down and look through them. Some of the kids can read but most of them are too young, so I read to them about deserts and polar seas and jaguars and tractors and Soviet combine harvesters, because that's the kind of books L has, and it doesn't actually matter what we're looking at, as long as there's something, something whole, a thing the kids can point at, so they can ask their questions, always new questions, so basic, so simple, and yet still I can't answer; I make things up and they believe me, since they have no one else to turn to, and we crouch in front of the tin walls and draw round the patches of paint with a thin marker pen, making a map of the world; they get to name the continents, they choose *Ear*, *Puddle*, they call the countries *Dogland*, *Sandia*, *The Isle of Swan*, *Slimeland*, we draw boats and fish and mountains and rivers, and we build bridges and motorways and cities, and the children, these morsels of humanity, each get their own city, their own country, and now I'm at war with you, they say, I'm bringing in my tanks and aircraft and subs, I'm bombing your cities so everyone dies, they say, I'm building my prison here and it's as big as your capital city so there's space for everyone, I'm putting barbed wire here so you can't get past, mines, missiles, grenades, and now I'm at war with you too and now the tin wall is completely covered with thin black traces of life and death and it's getting hard to play.

It never ends. I don't understand it, but every night when I close my eyes I picture it, suicide, in countless variations. The barrel of a rifle up against the roof of a mouth, the blade cutting the carotid artery, a cable wound round a throat and a feeling of weight, a jerk. Thoughts about what happens to a body, how much is left after it has put itself in the way of an oncoming train. The plastic bag, seen from the inside, the moisture, or a panicked inhalation, filling my lungs with water. Or the drugs, the poison, the medicine breaking down in my stomach and gradually starting to take effect. Rat poison is the worst, I've heard, because it takes effect so slowly, so the rats have time to spread it, to take it back to their nests, into their homes, give it to their family members and babies, it's meant to be very painful, a bad idea, at least that's what I've heard. L has a book with the title *Catastrophe*, and in it I read about the relationship between suicide, geography and climate, about differences between the sexes, different age groups, socio-economic factors, chains of cause and effect, cultures, nationalisation and internationalisation, images, maps with different colours to represent the frequency of suicides in different counties; Gotland, for instance, is completely black, but that has nothing to do with me, or the pieces of paper, the children's or mine, *I don't like sleeping* and *I never sleep cause sleep is the cousin of death*. I'm at L's, in his hut, reading about suicide, while the riots rage a few hundred metres away. I should be here making notes, reflecting on what's happening, keeping myself updated. I should document the abuses of the military, try to put the desperation into words, try to understand it, analyse the situation, really *understand*. I should try to stay awake, to take a sober look at things, my thoughts should be clearer, the reports even weightier. Three months have passed since I came here. Nothing's been written, the debts are mounting, and now here I am at L's, reading about the one thing I didn't want to think about. I remember how I described my first impression of this place in my notebook: 'It looks organic somehow, as though the little alleyways, huts and tents had grown up from the ground on their own, without any human involvement. The cables – thrown up arbitrarily between crooked posts and fences, over doorways, in and out of poorly covered windows, over water-soaked rag-rugs and cardboard boxes – look like they've draped themselves of their own accord, and the mortal danger they pose to everyone in their vicinity seems like something incomprehensible, or even innocent. When it rains, sparks drift down over the muddy soup. The kids who walk about out here move like adults, it's funny to watch their perambulations – four or five years old, they march along at a brisk pace, focused, busy with God knows what errand, hands in pockets, with faces that radiate earnestness, and if they meet a little comrade, they stop to exchange information with this same earnest expression. That's how it looks, businesslike, just so. Doing favours, returning them? Carrying things? Running and fetching them? But what, in this muck, other than the day's food and water rations? And the smell. Mould and urine, faeces and burnt plastic. It took a few days to grow accustomed to it. Not until it had taken over my own body and clothes did it fade from my consciousness. And I don't know if it's because I stopped caring or if it was by necessity, because it's not possible to escape the filth, and I'm not sure how to put it, but we've all – everyone, and everything – become *one.*'

A scrap of paper tumbles out of one of the books, it falls to the ground, I pick it up, turn it over, and see a pencil drawing of a baby's face, and I read: *The exploded and sewn-together heads of the children.* S, one of the children, finds the scrap of paper. How ugly, she says of the baby, and sounds out the line about the children's heads, then she reads it again and laughs crudely, calls the others and shows them and reads it to them. When I ask her what's so funny, she refuses to answer, but when I press her she says: *You're the one who's funny.*

It's the adults who fight. The men. First they stand, flexing their muscles in the sunshine, and when the sun goes down, they use their muscles, and if their muscles aren't enough they reach for the knives and handguns. The children look on, making a game of it; the moment you try to educate one of these barely one-metre-tall urchins, they're sticking imaginary guns in your face and pulling back the slide. But the big men are not playing, they actually shoot each other. Not a day passes without a shooting or an explosion or the smell of burnt human flesh sweeping in through the doorway.

L talks of his love for the children, he does everything he can for them and is crushed every time someone hurts them. It happens quite often, he says, and when they're sick he takes care of them. When S started vomiting violently a while back, he says, I held back her hair so it wouldn't get caught in the mess that was pouring from her mouth, and I whispered words of comfort, it felt strange and out of place. The cramps spread through her body and I promised her everything would be OK. I know this might sound rich coming from me, I said to her, but just get it out. And I told L everyone knows that's what you say – that if you can just get out all the sickness, all the poison, if you can rid yourself of the bad stuff, life can continue, and you say it even though you know it's not true, that it doesn't matter, because there'll always be something new.

When the images dissipate and I fall asleep, it's like I'm dead, I don't think I've ever slept so much; I can sleep ten, twelve hours and then I lurch around L's hut like a zombie, speechless and numb, sluggish, but somehow aggressive too. I drink L's energy drinks, then the kids come. I play with them and I come to life.

L has a folder of unnumbered sheets of paper he's printed out; around a hundred in total. On the first page it says: *This is for anyone who has neither the time nor the inclination to read the whole manual. A list of the twelve most effective and actionable methods (given that we live in Sweden). 1. Pentobarbital or other barbiturates (sleeping pills). 2. Opiates or drug cocktails. 3. Hanging. 4. Helium. 5. Train or metro. 6. Jumping from a high place. 7. Drowning. 8. Bleeding out. 9. Plastic bag over the head. 10. Gun. 11. Dehydration. 12. Hypothermia (freezing to death).* I don't know who wrote this list and I can't judge its accuracy. When I ask L about the folder he just shrugs and says there was a time before the crash when he printed out as much as he could and saved everything he came across, he had no idea what was what. That's how it was, he says, but he can't remember anything else. He doesn't want to talk about it. I look through his folders and read.

I can't stop thinking about how the children seemed to love lines like *The exploded and sewn-together heads of the children*, and how they would switch from irreproachable to reprehensible in the blink of an eye. I've heard people say the future is nestled inside children in a way that's reminiscent of unhatched chicks or butterflies, or silkworms and their cocoons. And it's for this reason that a dead child – a child cannot die! – is downright incontrovertible: death and the child form the strongest of all imaginable pairings, the most enduring of all, and perhaps that's why the kids liked those lines about the exploded and sewn-together child. Seeing that image makes them somehow stronger, even stronger, similarly to when a person has been dead but is revived: they say that, after experiencing death, that person may carry with them a greater knowledge of life than someone who's encountered only the one side of life, the living part, since they say – in a way reminiscent of that speech about chicks and butterflies and silkworms – that death is a part of life, and so we ourselves become children, and since we become children in relation to death, we are coupled with death, this enduring coupling, and at that moment we catch sight of the child's perceptions of the moment, the fear, and the longing for death, this whole image you create for yourself of the afterlife as you – in a fever, or in the process of fall-ing asleep, or in the back seat of your parents' or nanny's car – are gripped by a sense that you've in some way caused someone else's death; you ask peculiar questions of the person in the front seat, you imagine that death is like a journey, that you can come back from it, you act in irrational ways, like keeping half a sandwich to put it on the dead person's grave; you fantasise about how death affects the dead person in a purely physical sense, you wonder whether the dead person will have a thick beard upon their return, or float across the floor, slightly transparent, and you start to understand that you have to protect those close to you from death, because you realise that what can happen to *one* person can also happen to another, and later you also realise that death is final and universal, and that you can't link any one person's death with your own actions, that no one dies because you've stolen some sweets, for instance, and it's first and foremost the realisation that the dead person is not going to return that is painful and hard to deal with, at least until you've broadened your perspective a little as you experience the child dying inside you, and in time you come to realise that death is a natural part of life, or it should be, it used to be – a constant presence in a very tangible way in families, in homes, in society – at least in Catholic countries, for example, or countries with a Catholic culture, they say; many small details form a whole, for example how you relate to death and the dying, for the most part people die in their homes, it's normal to have a vigil with the dead person lying in repose, in their own bed, in their home, neighbours and friends come for the wake, for conversation, prayer, song and so on, and during the funeral service the casket is open and people come up to the dead person and kiss the dead person, but even in other places, in other cultures, people say that children are given the tools to deal with evil, suffering and death, including through the archetypal figures that symbolise that side of life in fairy tales; that's why fairy tales are necessary, they say, even if some fairy tales are about socially disadvantaged or sick children, who find the solutions to their problems not in this life but in dying alone, isolated and abandoned, like that little match girl, and they say that the lines between this life and the life beyond are porous in an unhealthy way, and it doesn't matter if the child is rich or poor – that is, whether they come from a rich family or a poor family – they say that social problems exist across all class divides, or that there are problems in every family, for every child, that's why they like the image of the sewn-together child's head, it helps, it soothes, for a moment at least, it becomes easier to sleep, it sounds strange but is supposed to be true, I guess it's about getting rid of preconceived ideas and the indoctrination of the social machine, society's psychological torture, you have to break free from all the ideas and concepts or they'll break you down; you can never become a butterfly, they say, unless you were first a caterpillar, and it's society that is the butterfly while a person – the child or an adult – is the cocoon; you can only lose, there is no resistance, or if there is it's futile, suicide is

99

not resistance, the thought of it is a futile resistance, if you can wish you'd never been born you've taken the first step, they say, you're a transmitter, you're projecting, you're sending children out to war in order that they might sleep at night, you're slicing off their eyelids to stop them crying, you're cutting off their genitals to bring them comfort; that's why the children think of lines like *The exploded and sewn-together heads of the children*, and that's why their switch from irreproachable to reprehensible happens in the blink of an eye, and that's the very reason the word 'child' exists, and when we say the future is nestled in a child's brain in a way that's reminiscent of an unhatched chick or butterfly, or silkworms and their cocoons, eggs, caterpillars, larval masses, it's to console ourselves, we know full well that it's not true: it's an imaginative construction, a feint.

What was it I wanted then? What did I want to achieve? I can no longer relate to the altruism that presumably motivated me, there's nothing left of it. I just look at the children here and I'm surprised; I've got stuck in one position and I can't stop, just as the thoughts of suicide have got stuck. Self-annihilation is another word for it. You climb up to a high spot, a bridge for example, a mountain or a building, and you jump, and I've learned now that the height must be at least forty-five metres over land, ten to twelve floors if there are tower blocks available, and seventy-five metres over the sea, otherwise it can have undesired consequences in terms of unpredictable and permanent injuries. Bridges are good because there's less risk of hitting a person. I've read about people landing on innocent passers-by, where the suicide has survived while the passer-by died, leading to the imprisonment of the former for manslaughter. You also avoid subjecting others to grotesque and potentially traumatic sights. Slice and dice is another thing I found out about – when you jump off a bridge but make something more of it. You need a high bridge, some rope and piano strings. You cut the ropes and the piano strings to different lengths, the piano strings have to be shorter than the ropes and all lengths must be shorter than the height of the bridge, you tie one end of each of the ropes and piano strings to the bridge, then you tie the other end of the ropes to various parts of your body – thighs, calves, arms, torso; and then you also tie the piano strings to your limbs, and when you jump off the bridge the different parts of your body are sliced off by the piano strings, but are held up by the ropes. However much I want to, I can never escape that image. The jolt, the decisive moment. But I'm never the one being dissected. Or am I? And who is it if it's not me? That part is vague, I have to admit, I have to say to myself, you're being a little vague now, not the image – that's clear as can be, powerful, you might say – but you, you're obscure, you lack definition and are therefore weak, unless it's the case that your power resides on another level, for example in the fact that suicide is not only a way of distancing oneself from one's own life but also, perhaps primarily, from a given situation, from a social situation, from society, from demands, from desires, both external and internal, but what, then, are these notions I have, these performances, films, sometimes image-less, and most often in a waking state, just before sleep – natural sleep, and not the kind tempted forth by barbiturates, ones that depress the central nervous system in descending order, beginning in the cerebral cortex, with sedation that leads to unconsciousness, and in an overdose, this leads to deep sedation and the cessation of breathing, because of the suppression of the respiratory centre, which is followed by cardiac arrest, they say, and sleeping pills are a really gentle method that's not the least bit uncomfortable, they say, at least if you succeed and don't wake up in a hospital, and one of the most common methods is sleeping pills washed down with alcohol, and you can put an airtight plastic bag over your head and an elastic band round your throat, to be on the safe side, and you can open the capsules and dissolve the contents in water so you don't vomit up the drug, which should ideally have a lasting effect, be strong, stable in solution with water, and cheap – the relaxant sodium pentobarbital fulfils these criteria and is the most commonly used, even if others, such as secobarbital, are acceptable, they say – of course it all depends on the dose, and the determination with which you plan and carry out the whole thing, you have to do it right from the beginning, so you don't have to do it again, go back to square one, you don't have to have your stomach pumped, which is a horrendous experience, they say, presumably – though of course there's no way of knowing – worse than death, and in *Catastrophe!* (the subtitle is *The Geography and Anthropology of Disaster*) I read that it all comes down to seismic changes, reversals, and the authors quote from the *National Encyclopaedia*, which mentions a great disaster with huge material destruction, after which people have difficulty imagining a return to or a continuation of previous conditions, and people talk about disasters as a painful or tragic event or situation: plane crashes, pandemics or meteor strikes, and it makes me feel ashamed but I can't say why, perhaps because I don't understand, but it is hard to understand, they say, we've learned to shut out the worst kinds of thoughts, and maybe it's not about images, maybe we have to leave behind this obsession with the visual, maybe instead it's about the notions we entertain, the concepts, the worst ones, I don't know, but maybe that's how it is, maybe it's rooted in something as simple as a notion of powerlessness, a sense of being totally, completely exposed, without a hint of any possibility of influencing a situation, without the slightest little possibility of even being able to imagine how you might influence a situation; they say that we make certain movements before we've had time to think about making them, so the movement makes itself, or the body does, the thing that accommodates both the self and the movement; they say that we *are lived*; they say that the experience of control, the experience of power, of agency, is a chimera, that it can't be true, that it's impossible, and that one might talk about needs and urges and desires, and survival instincts that exist on a level we can't perceive, but still they're so powerful they take over everything, they cause these catastrophes, change things, revolutionise, and this, my body, what is it really but a skein of yarn, a tangle of gestures, cumulative feedback loops, data being fed in, images again, of knives to cut open and break open the twists, the garrotte that constricts around my throat; I don't understand, I can't interpret what I'm seeing, perhaps it comes down to a happening, an occurrence, a chain of events, and, in that case, perhaps the images, even if they're compulsive, constitute a kind of antidote, create a state in which we're faced with the worst things, the most horrific things, but in this case they arise from our own imagination, or ability to conjure up notions, our own mind, the motor of our thoughts, and, consequently, we're not only exposed, we are also sovereign, in our own worlds of flickering sensory impressions, our own realities, steeped in terror, and maybe it's true that all this is disrespectful to those who are truly oppressed, a privilege, maybe I should say nothing more on the matter, nothing more about the things that weigh me down. Perhaps it's as simple as that.

PURITY

Kunegunda

And then there was the one who wanted to tell her children about how it felt to clean discotheques in the eighties. About the exhaustion, the lack of sleep. The particular smell of the toilets. The sticky bar. The cigarette butts and vomit on the floor. Sometimes blood. Used condoms. The traces of amphetamine and cocaine. The way the body reacts to all this then gradually refuses. Until it becomes impossible. The children already know about the sick notes. The empty days. The complete paralysis. The ashtrays and the sleepiness and the bills and the drawn-out greyness that feels so banal, so clichéd it should be unreal, easier to sweep away and shine a light into. But it's not an option. It exists, hard and unavoidable. Like in those films she loathed, those British kitchen sink dramas, full of misery and poverty and people suffering and struggling and toiling. Mostly to no effect, because it wouldn't have been realistic if they'd succeeded at anything. Then it would have been like it is in those American rags-to-riches films and they were even worse. That lie: if X can succeed, so can you – or worse still was when *the star themselves* started bleating: If *I* can do it, so can *you* – that felt like a great big gob of spit in the face every time. These days, this was the kind of thing (metaphorical bodily fluids rather than real ones) that made Kunegunda, or Kinga as her friends called her, feel really ill. So no, better to watch something else. Animal documentaries, for instance. Monkeys in particular she liked to watch, or fish or ants.

How is it possible, she often thought as she lay there in front of the TV, relaxed and yet not, happy and yet not, how is it possible that humanity is so impoverished and blinkered, when nature is so rich in perspective. The nature programmes are one long performance of colour and form, there are so many different ways to live, it's almost impossible to comprehend, and that's in spite of the fact that there is still so much we know nothing about, high above us and deep below. Compare this to the history programmes that are nothing but a repetition of the same pattern, again and again. She found humanity repulsive in its poverty. But sometimes she inclined to a thriller or detective novel too. Ideally one in which the violent men, the johns and the high-ranking murderers, got banged up in the end – she liked that kind of unreality. From reality you could expect nothing but injustice and oppression. Everyone licks upwards and kicks downwards. One way or another. No exceptions.

She would like to tell her children all of this. Straight to the point, no minimising it, or dressing it up in apologies and phrases that undermined her own experiences and memories and feelings and thoughts. Later, when it was said, once this basic thing was formulated, manifest, then she would add nuance, clarify things. Because of course there were exceptions. Cleaning schools, for instance, was different. At least there you got a glimpse of the life you were missing. The life that was inaccessible, lost. I started my shifts early there, she would like to say, and just as I was finishing, life began to stream in. Head teacher, janitor, teachers, all the other staff who were there during the day, all the people who made the cogs turn. Then came the children. The movement, the noise. The eyes. All the joy that seemed to somehow confirm a truth I didn't want to see or concede. I don't know what I mean by that. I don't know, she wanted to say, I don't know. Or maybe I do know, but I can't say. I'm mute.

And it's true. She can't say it, can't formulate it. But it exists. (Because it exists in the words, surely? Hidden? Only to burst forth in different forms: your hard work in the wake of other people's hedonism and freedom? Your own capacity for pleasure . . . your potential epicureanism, smothered. No, she can't say it, can't formulate it. But it exists. Or, does it exist? Or, it exists, does it?)

Simone
But in the morning, while I was cleaning up after the night before, it occurred to me we'd actually been conditioned to admire these people – the musicians, poets, artists, bohemians and drug addicts. Antisocial people, criminal people and their so-called 'freedom'. That it was our parents who passed on this fascination, this attraction to self-destruction. An infantile, puerile idea that the goal of growing up is to destroy yourself and your life. When I grow up I'll become an artist and kill myself, as my brother said when he was six.

A name
Because my thoughts are interrupted by a knock at the door. I put my cup of coffee down on the windowsill, pause my music, go over to the door and open it. It's the cleaner standing there. She looks me in the eye and says hello but quickly looks down. I want to say that no, there's no cleaning needed today, but when she makes a move to come into the room I take a step back and instead mumble something inaudible. The cleaner doesn't say anything, she goes over to the waste paper basket and takes out the virtually empty plastic bag, ties it, and puts in a new one. I walk indecisively over to the window, my eyes catching on her throat and the curve of her breasts and say, *Er, yeah, OK,* picking up my cup. I look out the window at the same time as I take a sip and realise the coffee has gone cold. The cleaner leaves the room with the rubbish bag and comes back in with a red bucket, cleaning fluid, a window squeegee and a variety of cloths. I walk over to the coat rack and take a pocket diary out of the inside pocket of my coat. I flick through it distractedly and then get out my phone. The time is 11.06. It's a little early to be eating lunch, but maybe it would be best to get it over and done with, so I can get more work

done in the afternoon. I turn towards the cleaner, who's started on the windows. Yeah, that's what I'll do, I think, now mildly irritated. She interrupted me, and that is irritating. I turn again, put on my coat, walk over to the desk and pick up my laptop, putting it in my briefcase and saying, *Can you lock up later, I'm going.* She turns to me. *I'm going to have lunch soon,* I add. She looks at me, a little too long I think. I get the sense her eyes are entirely black. Is she slow, does she not understand Swedish? Then she nods and says, *Yes,* turns and goes on working. I leave the room.

Ferreira
But is it physical, he wonders, fastening a catch on the feeder, tightening the cable, opening a hatch and checking the hydraulic cylinder, and thinking that it will work out, I have to believe everything will work out, somehow it's going to work out. Nothing wrong here, business as usual. Some people are so much fucking worse off. I'm fine, we're lucky, in many ways. There's a hiss and he shuts the hatch and releases the catch and presses the little green square, and he feels the doubt as an actual physical substance in his chest and shoulders, and he thinks about alcohol and he knows that it will soon be time for a meeting, at last.

Another name
Or, to be precise: it's now, as you're cleaning the toilet a stranger has emptied their upset bowels into, that you really start questioning whether the decision to leave what you had in search of something better was really the right one. How do you recognise necessity? Do you remember what your mother said: Why is it some people are never content with what they have?

Rafael
But I've told my daughter how I used to sit on the balcony when I couldn't sleep, used to sit and smoke cigarettes, stricken with

anxiety because I couldn't stop thinking how *right now, right in this moment* – in 'the European night', as we used to say when we worked night shifts, as I sat there in silence, waiting for the sun to come up so I could fill my water bottle with vodka, put it in the bag with my other tools, get on my bike and head off for yet another working day in which windowpane after windowpane had to be cleaned and polished, cleaned and polished, cleaned and polished (you can't say it just once, that would be unreasonable, unrealistic, unworthy) – that *in this very moment* literally hundreds of millions of people in China were on their way to work in factories, hundreds of millions, that is to say several hundred times a thousand, times thousands, it ought to be a fiction; as if one's own reluctance and lack of enthusiasm about one's work were multiplied and raised to a feverish level; the man in the handbag shop who laughed in my face when I asked him which bags weren't made in China . . . My dear friend, he said, *everything* is made in China. And that line in a song that struck me: *If everything is made in China, are we Chinese?* You and your tattoos, I say to my daughter, why don't you all get tattoos that say 'I am Chinese':

Yet another name
And then maybe someone will help you.

Forgotten name
Plus that time I was working the bar at a company party – a kind of *happy hour deluxe* – it was a free bar, and these young, well-dressed, arrogant, self-assured business people got very drunk, very quickly. At one point this guy came over to the bar and told me to mix gin, vodka, bourbon and rum in a big glass, top it up with Guinness and lager, a few splashes of Tabasco and then finish up with a few crumbled Pringles. I did as he asked and then gave him the drink, which he tried to down in one, while his buddies stood there laughing their heads off and the women shook their heads, without being able to conceal how impressed and attracted they were by his dickishness. But he failed and had to put down his glass after two thirds. He was standing by the bar, nursing his nausea, while I walked over to the till and entered everything twice, just as we'd been ordered to. I even entered and mixed an extra Long Island Iced Tea, which I took out into the little storage area behind the bar without anyone noticing. I lit a cigarette, drank my cocktail in a couple of big gulps, and watched a spider slowly climbing around in a corner of the ceiling.

After a while, the Pringles guy puked all over the floor. I went and got a mop and bucket. When I came over to the vomit and was about to start mopping, the guy was standing there with his boss, a woman in her fifties. She told him to mop it up himself. I saw straight away that the little bastard wouldn't be able to manage it – he could barely stand – so I said I'd sort it out. No, said the guy's boss. I want him to do it. She took the mop out of my hands and gave it to the guy, who dunked it in the bucket and pulled it out again. With a splashing, slapping sound he put the wet mop down right on the vomit, which went from being a viscous mess, spread over a square foot or so, to a runny soup spread right across the floor. That doesn't look right, the boss said. Have you never learned to clean up after yourself? The guy made a second attempt, making a couple of violent, sweeping movements that spread out the slop even more. No, no, no, she said, totally useless. You're totally useless. The guy lifted the mop, dripping and splashing while his buddies laughed. Fucking waste of space, they said, shouting over each other. I looked at them, everything seemed so forced. The boss wore a tight smile, it looked as though she was literally in pain but was still enjoying it. She was silent for a few long seconds and then she looked at me, and I knew exactly what she was going to say.

Insignificant name

So, like, bodily fluids and that. One time I picked up two old guys who started going on about how one of them had done a real number on a hotel room. They were imagining how shocked the chambermaid must have been when she came into the bathroom and saw the faeces spread all over the place. I didn't say anything but thought she probably wouldn't have been all that shocked. Tired, but not surprised. And probably glad she didn't have to see them do it. Or something even worse. Another time I went along to a friend's hotel room. It was a mess, a real pig-sty. And I knew his home wasn't like that. Not that he was overly anal or anything, but he kept it clean and tidy and nice. I didn't say anything to him either, but after that I didn't like him as much. If I stay in a hotel I usually clean the room before I leave, and I always hang the 'Don't Disturb' sign throughout my stay, so the person cleaning has less to do. Though one time a cleaner asked me to take the sign off so she could get in to clean it. She got paid for each room she cleaned and everyone in the hotel had had their signs hung up for several days, which meant she'd hardly made anything that week. Clean it if you want, I said to her. But it was already clean. Because I clean the room myself. Once a day I take a bit of paper, or a sock that's been worn, moisten it and use it to wipe all the surfaces. I check the sheets for stains. I try to gather all my rubbish in one place, either in or by the bin, and I'm particularly careful about the toilet, so there's no blood or snot or any other kind of mess visible. I clean away any hairs, clean the drain in the shower and scrub the toilet bowl with the toilet brush. I don't want anyone to have to touch anything that's been inside my body. The hotel room should be clean and fresh when I leave. No trace left. Nothing.

Difficult name
And I wish I could understand their language, she thought as she turned her back to them and bent down to pick up Lego bricks from the floor, a language that's my language too.

Lionel
Because then my mum's friend sorted me out with a job. It was in a bingo hall. It was me and Lionel – I was like sixteen and he was maybe thirty. We were supposed to polish the floor. We got there in the evening and we were due to work half the night. It was a pretty big place, maybe 200 square metres or something. So many tables. And chairs. They had to be moved back and forth between the different bits of the hall. The tables were all sticky underneath. This gross brown muck from all the cigarettes, cigarillos and pipes people smoked. Then we turned the polishing machines on. I can't remember all the different elements, but it was like vacuum, scrub, wax and polish. There was quite a bit of dead time while the chemicals were doing their thing or drying. So we'd go and eat or sit on the floor of a hall where the floor didn't need cleaning. We ate sandwiches and pick n mix and drank Pepsi, one of those three-litre bottles that don't exist any more, or at least I haven't seen them for ages. We drank out of blue coffee cups. Lionel asked me loads of stuff about what it was like to be young these days. If I went out a lot. About alcohol, drugs, girls. I thought he was a bit much. But then he started telling me about how he lost his virginity. He was fourteen, living in some little dump in Skåne. He'd been drinking moonshine with friends and they were really drunk, hanging out in a

park. Listening to music, smoking. They met a couple of older girls, nineteen-year-olds who'd been at a bar. The girls teased them and joked around. Little boys, little lads, want to come and fuck, they said. Sure, the boys had replied. And Lionel went off with one of them. She kept teasing him because he was so little and because he was an immigrant. Don't you have any big brothers, she said. Don't you have any cousins where you come from? I've never fucked a darkie. She asked if he was a virgin and he lied. Course I'm not. She didn't believe him. They got back to her place and drank more. Over her bed, she showed him, she had a big poster for her boyfriend's band, a hard rock band. Where is he now then? Lionel asked. Fuck knows, she said. Probably screwing groupies somewhere. Then she grabbed hold of Lionel, pushed him down onto the bed and straddled him. He lay there, looking at the poster, and later, when she'd undressed, at her big breasts. I sucked them and tried to feel happy, he said. But he felt sick and started worrying about STIs and pregnancy, so he took out a condom he'd had in his wallet for over a year. He'd been given it by his brother when he turned thirteen. You're a teenager now, bro, time you got laid. But you have to be careful, believe me; you don't want to get AIDS and you don't want to have a kid. Now he took out the dry, wrinkled condom. She laughed and threw it away. You don't shower with rubber boots on, do you? she said. Then she started sucking his floppy cock. Lionel felt dizzy and sick, and he looked at the poster for the hard rock band behind her. I remember thinking, he said, it's obvious those guys are geeks trying to look hard. I wanted to fight them. She went on sucking and then started riding him. He felt sick and wanted to stop, but couldn't. He just licked her breasts and tried to get hard. The phone rang at one point. She got up and answered it. Someone was asking where she was and what she was doing. I'm fucking a darkie, she answered. Then she hung up and carried on. After a while, Lionel crashed out. When he woke the next morning there were two other people in the room. They were joking with the girl about how she'd deflowered a child, that it was illegal. Lionel got dressed quickly and left. He was disappointed. With the fucking, which he'd imagined would be fun. And with his cock, which hadn't got hard. With himself, because he was too little. Then the girl had got hold of his number somehow. And rung in the middle of the night, woken his mum up. Called her a whore when she refused to pass the receiver to Lionel, who was sleeping. It was a school night. And then his mum had said to Lionel: Who are these sluts you're hanging out with? Lionel laughed when he said that. Then he went to check on the floor. He said it was dry enough. We put the last coat of polish on and turned out all the lights. Just watch out for scabby sluts, he said as we left. I had a hard time getting to sleep because of all the Pepsi we'd drunk. But I got a few hours and then he picked me up again in his car. It was obvious he hadn't slept much either and he stank of booze. We drove to the bingo hall, did another round of polishing. Then we took off and ate breakfast before moving the tables and chairs back. It was fucking disgusting, that sticky stuff on the undersides. After a while our hands were covered in it, it smelled like shit, like ashtray and old man's mouth. But the floor was perfectly clean, it glistened like water in front of us. As though covered with a very thin, delicate sheet of ice.

Seb
But then the eighteen-year-old said to Seb: 'One day you're going to work for me. Scum.'

Seppä
Or maybe you think you've already heard it all? But have I told you about the guy I met in Helsinki, the one who disinfected apartments after unusually messy suicides? You don't want to know all the sick things he told me . . . or maybe you do. Maybe you want me to recount it all, in exhaustive detail yet calmly and collectedly. With a kind of dignity and respect for everyone involved. And for myself? But no.

I don't want to go into the details. To be honest though, it did sound like everything was true. Yeah, it was spectacular and everything, but I mean, someone has to do that job, there are like two suicides a day in Finland, even though what they say about Finland being the land of suicide is apparently a myth, and, yeah, someone has to clean up the apartments afterwards, don't they? You weren't expecting the cops to do it? The fire service? No, they're honourable, middle-class fellows – climbers, you know, hard-working people. The kind of guys who want *honour* and *hero status*, they want to go home to their *well-kept houses* where their *wives* have cooked a *healthy meal*. They want to take a shower, shave their scrotum and get an early night so they're fresh for their morning run in the park, they don't want to stand around with other people's innards in their nostrils, to have to stand over the sink in the evening, picking all that dry stuff out of their noses, you know, that last bit of dust, those little crusts that always get stuck inside your nostrils however many face masks you've been wearing; they don't want to have that smell in their noses when they're going to sleep and, you know, start thinking about *what it is*, and not be able to sleep because they keep thinking about *what it is* and *what it was* that drove that person to put an *end* to it all. They don't want to know about that stuff. So it falls to him, and people like him. His background, according to him: butcher's son. Combat pilot. Had 'problems' after an accident. A couple of 'difficult years' with 'a lot of coming and going and toing and froing'. My reading: he caused an accident and was given a jail sentence. He came out, but had nothing left and addiction took over. Pretty basic story. At first he acted tough and that, said it was no trouble, just something you got used to, but then, after a load of beers and a few shots of vodka I bought him, he admitted there was a trick to dealing with it. I just pretend I'm cleaning the slaughterhouse after my dad's been working. And I think about the animal, the pig or the calf or the cow or whatever it is. I think hard, intensely, about the animal. I think only about the animal, not the person. Not about the person at all.

Never about the person. You get it? *Ei koskaan.* There are no humans, only animals. The animal's flesh is not like a human's. The animal's blood . . . the animal's soul . . . it's a whole other thing. It's just the animal and me here, he said, and actually, I'm an animal myself.

Your names
And that it shouldn't get turned into some kind of exaggerated regard for economic hygiene, you know?

Apolonia
So on Friday I was off for the first time in eleven days. I had a lie-in and it was nice, though my shoulders felt stiffer than usual. My data had run out, so I borrowed William's laptop and downloaded the new playlist onto my phone. It was sunny. I cycled round the park, listening to the music. I was happy and really wanted to go dancing again. Went to the charity shops – Myrorna first, and then the Red Cross shop, Erikshjälpen and finally Emmaus. I was looking for bedsheets – I've only got one left since I accidentally ripped a massive hole in the blue one. I couldn't sew it up, it was already too thin. I found a white double for twenty kronor and a pair of Nike Air Monarchs for thirty. They smelled a bit and were worn in a weird way on the heels. But I thought I could give them a good wash and put something in under the insole. Actually, they almost looked new. I checked online later and saw they would have cost more than 1,000 kronor, so I've really earned something. The sheet was in good nick too, and probably cost several hundred new. It felt pretty luxurious too. So I went home feeling pleased with how the day had gone. Then I met Ghada. We walked down to the sea and checked out the people and the houses and cars. Then in the evening there were some TV programmes I'd been meaning to see – William had downloaded whole seasons for me. FaceTimed with my baby and said good night. Slept well. A pretty good day, in other words.

One more name

And one night I noticed how hard she was trying not to start bawling as she pushed her way between the tables, collecting glasses and emptying ashtrays. I went over to her by the dishwasher a while later and asked what had happened.

'Nothing,' she said.

'Are you sure? I can see you're unhappy. Has something been going on?'

And it turned out a young guy at one of the tables had felt her up. Touched her thighs and breasts. Juan, who was standing there next to us, got all aggravated and wanted us to take the guy down to the basement and *show him what happens.* But we couldn't, so Mohammed just sent the security guard over, who calmly and matter-of-factly told the guy to leave the bar. He played all innocent, but he was grinning as he threw a note on the table and put on his blazer.

The same name

And on the way home, on the train, she formulated a few things she would say to her brother: I wish there was a scene I could call upon to illustrate my experience of class. A putatively pithy and unambiguous scene where some boss hits or spits at my parents in front of me. Or better still, where the boss's children humiliate my parents. First me, then my parents who refuse to get involved. But there are no such scenes. Even if it has happened, at least in a metaphorical sense. Metaphorical gobs of spittle. The realisation that other people, adults as well as children, can humiliate your parents is one of the first clues you're given as you're growing up. And that it often leads to your parents taking it out on you, in one way or another, consciously or unconsciously, intentionally or unintentionally. It. And who do you take *it* out on? That's a question you have to answer, even as a child. Everyone who knows about life there – with us, among us, around us – knows the worst of it is what we inflict on ourselves. We beat and humiliate, or simply neglect and undermine, our children, we oppress our sisters, we abuse and kill our brothers. The only reason there's so much talk of loyalty between us is that we have to work hard to hide the fact it's so cheap, so easily bought. Most people will do anything for the opportunity to go and feel inferior at middle-class cocktail parties. I remember a sentence from one of your books, where someone says that J. P. Morgan, the famous financier, once said he'd have no difficulty bribing one half of the working class to shoot the other half. In fact, that assertion was made by a rich nineteenth-century US landowner, Jay Gould, who said he'd be able to pay half the protesting agricultural labourers to shoot the other half. And it's basically still true today. And every single one of us participates in this by looking up to successful people, to the climbers, the 'diligent', 'competent' ones. By judging everything, every day, all the time – how good was that book, that summer, that evening in with the family. How smart is this person, how good is her daughter at maths, how good are we at judging what's best for us anyway? Bro, I'm just happy to be alive.

Redacted name
Though actually my name was changed. It was to protect me. That she changed it. The journalist, I mean. But even if my name had been my actual name, my name still would have been changed. In a way. It's a matter of transliteration. Do you know what I mean? Actually changed. In a way. And the sounds no one can pronounce. In the throat and on the tip of the tongue. Forget it. So your name has been changed too. You know? Everyone's names have been changed.

Hadgi
Because I had no job and no money and I didn't want to be at home, there were too many people there and too much trouble, so I sat in the basement of the library and it was so quiet and my whole body was rejoicing and I was flicking through three books at random, first one, then the other, then the first again, then the third; I would

read short passages here and there, skimming a little, jumping back and forth through the book, slowly, but, like, without resistance, and it calmed me down. I sank down in my chair, I thought loads of thoughts, many, many thoughts, like a spider web of thoughts, I thought, then I thought, no, that was dumb, that was a dumb idea, not a spider web, no, not a spider web, I don't know, but it was so nice down there, no people, no noise, just a distant hum, a radio playing music two floors up, and there was murmuring and bustling, I could hear my tinnitus, I could hear the sound of my shoe on the tiled floor as I moved my foot and it was so nice to not be at work, to just sit there with these books and flick back and forth, and think sort of thin, almost invisible thoughts, and I could feel my pulse, I felt my pulse and I heard a vacuum cleaner getting closer, and I looked around, saw the books, their colourful spines, the bookshelves, the walls, the ceiling, the lights, the whiteboard and the bone-white coffee cups in the corner, and I looked for spider webs but couldn't see any, and then I looked at the books and I did nothing, I sat and read, aimlessly, and it was nice, I closed my eyes a while, then I opened my eyes again and flicked through one of the books, then another, and then I noticed there was a fly sitting on the book, an insect, a little yellow bug, but it probably wasn't a spider, and I flicked it off with my middle finger and went on reading, and the vacuum cleaner fell silent and I could hear the radio and the hum again, and then that stopped too, and I could hear my tinnitus and I thought about the alphabetical order of the bookshelves and this is what I thought: imagine if there was a thread, a very thin thread, running from every book in here to the forehead of the person who wrote it, I wonder what that would look like, I wonder what kind of pattern that would make, I guess many of these writers are dead, maybe most of them are dead, but maybe the threads could travel through time somehow, in space-time, or whatever it's called, no, I don't know, that was a dumb idea, I thought, and I put the book down and looked at my hand, and thought about how it looked like a spider, three more fingers and it would have been a spider, I thought, and then I stood up, because it was time to go, the time had flown by, it was time to put the three books back and as I did this I had a thought, a thin, fluttering, almost invisible thought, that was somehow without origin: spiders have all the time in the world.

Double name

Like . . . that I never wear white underwear or pale shoes . . . that I put bleach on the stains and so on . . . so my skin gets irritated and weird . . . that I keep . . . polishing shoes and rubbing dirt off jackets . . . and caps . . . like mad, several times a day . . . that I go to the hairdresser more than necessary . . . that I brush my teeth . . . four times . . . a day . . . until my gums bleed . . . that I am constantly smoothing . . . and straightening . . . and brushing off . . . and polishing . . . and checking . . . That was what . . . that was what bothered her.

Vitali

Though you're not alone either, there's always new things coming up, new perspectives, new situations pop up the whole time to show you it's all much bigger than you think, you know. Like this one time, I was at a party, or more of a dinner actually, with a colleague, a boss, he was a successful academic, well-off, you know, big house, nice area, big family, big car, the whole lot . . . so we went out into the garden for a cigarette, he was pretty wasted, it was late, it was night-time, you could see the constellations, we were sitting in a hammock, and I guess I'd been spinning some yarn inside that he wanted a part of, so he started telling me about his childhood, his upbringing, and it was the usual stuff, you know, no money, poverty all around and parents who made everything worse and so on, and I said:

'I know, I know.'

And then he started talking about his sons, how they'd been mugged by some kids from another part of town, one of those so-called 'million project' districts nearby, which looked like the place where he'd grown up, and was the same place I'd once lived, and maybe that was why he could tell me all this, because suddenly he started weeping, right there in the hammock, he started sort of quietly crying, and then he told me that when this happened, when his kids and their friends got mugged, there'd apparently been a bit of a wave of muggings, he hadn't been able to support his children properly, to take care of them like he'd wanted to, because he'd identified more with the muggers, with the lads from the other district, you know, he'd felt some kind of anger, rage, or — he didn't say it, but even hatred — towards his own children.

That's what I mean. That's how it is. That's how it goes.

And we sat there. In the darkness, under the stars, in the hammock.

He was crying and I said: 'Of course, that's how it is.'

And he said: 'It's like a hole in my life.'

And I said: 'Of course, I know, I know.'

And he said: 'Like I'm just one big hole.'

And: 'Do you know what a hole is?'

And I said: 'Of course, a hole inside you, an emptiness in your life.'

And he said: 'No, a hole is nothing, it's something that doesn't exist, it's nothing. But still. You can still count the holes, right? If you have more than one hole you can count them, like: one hole, two holes, three holes, eight, nine, ten holes. And if you can count them, there has to be something, there must be something for you to count. So in the end it's like you don't exist, you know, you're alive and you're there, you can count the days, hours, minutes, you can count it all, it's there, you're a person, but at the same time you don't exist, you're nothing, if you disappeared it would make no difference, there'd just be a little less of everything.'

Adam

And then this: the others went into the peep show while I waited outside. Just waited, that was all.

Unpleasant name

But not that all-inclusive would include a buffet with pigs' faces. There were sliced pig faces, all in a row, maybe ten or fifteen slices of face, and when I looked closer – I couldn't help it – I saw that they were human faces, sliced off, or rather flayed, like masks, and I started to wonder if we were meant to wear them, if we were meant to perform in them, to put on some kind of performance for the other guests, the ones in the VIP lounge, or if we were meant to just eat them, to dip them in the pale green avocado crème that was in a milky-white, two-litre tub alongside them.

Familiar names

And one day the police did a raid at work and picked up A____ and G____, who were taken into custody, where they stayed for five and seven months respectively before being deported. After that I don't know what happened to them.

A few weeks later I got home from work and started making dinner. I'd put everything out, got the dessert ready, and sat down to eat, when my son suddenly said he wanted to be a policeman when he grew up.

I took half a potato and dipped it into the spinach stuffing, which tasted much too strongly of nutmeg. I remember thinking about that, that I never managed to strike the right balance of white pepper and nutmeg, at the same time as I considered what to say to my son.

I was already so fucking tired. And I knew it was a phase. He's only seven, I thought, there are things he doesn't understand. Things I have to protect him from – at least for a couple more years.

I said OK and nodded. We ate in silence. Then he added: 'Better than being a cleaner like you.'

So I sat him down at the computer and showed him clip after clip of police officers beating unarmed protestors with batons. Police firing rubber bullets at children. Policemen beating people in handcuffs. Police kicking people lying on the floor in the head and the back and the ribs. Police vehicles driving straight into crowds.

And so on.

More than an hour passed. I told him about the deportations, about A——— and G———. About the detention centre in Åstorp. About how I myself had been insulted and threatened by the police. I told him about police violence, about police racism, police misogyny. I repeated things my father had told me, stories from back home, things my mother had told me, things my grandfather had told me, things my aunt had told me.

'We're the little people,' I said. 'We've always been the little people.'

'The police are always on the side of power. Never on ours.'

I explained what a monopoly on violence is, described the relationship between state violence and the will of the little people to live, to survive.

I said: 'Countless people have been harassed and tortured and murdered by the police so that you and I wouldn't have to live as serfs.'

I told him about Sinthu Selvarajah and Osmo Vallo and the Baseball Gang and Eric Torell and Lenine Relvas-Martins and a load of other stories about police violence in Sweden, and read out one Wikipedia page after another. I showed him The Counted, the website that counts all the people who've been killed by the police in the US that year. The number that day was 1,088 – I think it was in early November. I asked him to calculate how many that was per month, per day.

'Is that the kind of thing you want to do?' I asked. 'Is it?'

I asked over and over again, and I didn't stop until he started crying and said he would never, ever join the police.

I held him for a long time. And then I gave him an extra-large portion of ice cream with chocolate sauce and roasted almonds.

Sara
That is, it's a question of basic psychology. It looks like strength, or it's intended to communicate strength, but it stems from weakness,

from a sense of inferiority and a fear of losing control of the situation.
One tip is to lose the sarcasm. It signals weakness, I think.

Yet another unknown name
But they weren't even my things. They were there when I arrived. It
wasn't my cup, or my plate, or my screwed-up napkin. But I cleared
them away because I didn't want the manager to think I was the one
who'd left them there (just like I clean up after other people in the
laundry room, because I'm the one they'll suspect if it's left in a mess).

Dilma
'But still,' she said. 'Most of us have a voice. And I don't mean a meta-
physical voice – neither existence nor history talks through us in that
way. And it's certainly not some desperate fantasy about democracy.'
    'What do you mean then?' I asked.
    'It's the body,' she said. 'It's lungs, vocal cords, a mouth, nose and
so on. The vocal apparatus, I think it's called. Yes, I believe the speech
therapists call it the vocal apparatus. Or the voice coaches. Have you
ever been to a voice coach?'
    'No,' I said.
    'I was sent to a voice coach when I was in secondary school,' she
said. 'I remember the room. The narrow, badly lit room where I was
forced to sit and read children's books with a woman who had such
bad breath it overpowered the smell of the cough sweets she was constantly sucking on. *Kalle has a ball, Lisa sings sweetly.* The humiliation
of someone teaching me to speak again. I was thirteen and I spoke
five languages. Not perfectly, and I mumbled a bit too much, a bit
too often. But still.'
    I laughed.
    'You laugh,' she said. 'Is it funny? Maybe. Yeah, the symbolism is
much too obvious, it's not particularly subtle. Perhaps that's why,' she
said. 'But still. How many times have I encountered similar stories?
Told to me by other immigrants and the children of immigrants whose

ability to communicate was called into question or otherwise viewed as "impure". Their descriptions of the "cleansing" process and the contempt it bred. I had a voice back then, but it was unintelligible. You have to pull yourself together, they said. Focus. You have to create clear, recognisable patterns if you want us to see you.'

Two names
And I've told you: this just isn't going to work. It isn't. They'll be here to get us soon.

Yeah. Like Mama used to say when we were little: 'If they take you away from me, just remember that I love you, remember that.'

For fuck's sake, stop it. What are we going to do?

Do? What are we going to do?

Admit it. You don't care.

I care . . . or don't care . . . it's all the same, no?

What's with you?

With me? What's with me?

Yeah, you're being illogical. What's with that?

Notes, yeah. Like, the memory of notes. Sound memories. Or like, a feeling.

Memories of sounds?

Yeah. Maybe. But short, chopped-up pieces. Words. Rhythms. Notes layered over one another in boxes. On shelves in factories. At night, when the night watchman is sleeping. He's crashed out over his iPad. His face is lit up by small lights. Orange, green. The red one is flashing. I'm wearing work clothes. Faint odour of sweat. Shoes with steel caps and some kind of cushioned sole. It's soft. It's really soft to walk on the hard, cold concrete floor. It's quiet, apart from the noise of the lights. Apart from this ticking and clicking. The machines, the tapes, the robot arms, the holes, the discharge valves. They're silent. I imagine a kind of shower of sparks over the whole thing. Like fireworks indoors.

Why aren't they on?

There's a few hours' wait between the night shift and the day shift. I don't know. Maybe the machines need to rest. To be lubricated, checked over. I don't know. Certain lights – in the corridor and by the loading bays – are never turned off. It's frightening. In the beginning it was also frightening that this work was going on all the time. Mostly I slept during those few hours of down-time. Otherwise it was like, at any time, when I wasn't working, I might suddenly think: the others are working right now. I could see them before me. I knew what they were doing. I could sense it. In some ways I was always there. I mean, it gets inside you somehow. Something to do with neural pathways, apparently. That's what someone said. He was going to be a doctor . . . I can't remember what he was called. Farzad or Farrokh or something. Now I'm going to put the coffee on and go out for a smoke. The smoking room is too gross. Makes me feel panicky, reminds me of the psych ward. I meet the cleaners in the kitchen. One of them smells of incense. We say hello, nothing more – only one of them speaks Swedish and he's not that chatty. They're heading to their next job – they work like twelve-hour shifts or something. I wish I had someone to talk to. I miss my friends. I feel . . . threatened, insecure.

Why are you alone?

The other guy, I don't want to say his name, came in drunk. He's in the locker room, sleeping it off. I'm covering for him. We're always covering for him. He's often drunk.

Why?

That's just how it is.

Was that how it was?

Yeah, it was. Precisely. I remember how it sounded when the lights went on in the factory. The fluorescent tubes. How many would there have been. Hundreds. Maybe thousands. I don't know. More than you could see. More than you could count. It was like a jingling sound. A clicking and then a humming noise that was sort of mixed with a shock. The eyes. The signals: light! Light! Light! . . . Factory! Soda factory. Soda. Soda pop, soda slop, soda soda soda. Life was that soda. Like: yeah. This is what my life tastes like. And there are little bubbles in it that float up to the top and burst.

Is that true?

The fuck you reckon? What else would it be? A lie?

What's the difference?

What do you mean? They're opposites. What do you mean, 'What's the difference?'

Aren't opposites just two sides of the same thing?

No.

Yeah, for real.

Now you're the one being illogical. I've heard . . . that the difference between a lie and the truth is that . . . that the lie . . . is sweet to begin with but bitter at the end . . . And the truth . . . is bitter to begin with but sweet in the end.

Sweat.

Sweat?

Sweet, I mean.

Sweet. Kind of sticky like spilled . . . undiluted . . . cordial, syrup, soda concentrate.

No. Pleasing. More like that.

Pleasant.

Yeah.

Pleasing.

Pleasing. You mean shady.

Yeah.

Real shady.

Exactly. Everything's shady.

The shadiest thing is that everything exists. I mean, think for a minute. Everything exists. *That* is shady.

Of course it exists. What do you mean?

No, but I mean, think about it. *Everything*, what is that? You get me? You have no way of knowing what it is because you haven't seen it. You've only seen your own life, right?

So you mean like other countries and shit?

Yeah. Countries, places, times, God. All the things you've never seen or heard or even thought about.

No, OK.

So you have no way of really knowing what you mean when you say everything, agreed?

I guess I mean everything I've seen. Or heard.

Yeah, but that's not everything. You just said so yourself.

No, OK. And?

And in that case you have no way of knowing what it means to *exist*. I mean, you know certain ways of existing, but not all of them, so you only know part of it, see what I mean?

I mean, everything exists in the same way, no?

What kind of everything? You yourself said you don't know what everything is.

No.

You get me?

No, I don't get anything. You might as well say nothing exists.

Yeah, you can say what you want. You can make anything up, talk your own language only you understand, but that doesn't mean it's true.

No, but it exists.

What?

Everything.

Now you're having a laugh.

You're the one having a laugh. You think too much.

What do you mean?

What do you mean, what do I mean? You think too much. You're thinking all wrong.

What do you mean, wrong?

Wrong. No one thinks like you do. No one talks like that. No one uses words like you do.

What are you talking about?

You know.

130

What? I just think the way I think. How should I talk then?

You know.

What?

What's up?

What do you mean, what's up?

What's up with you?

What's up with me? What's up with me, why am I so weird? Why am I different, why am I not normal, why am I sweet and sticky?

Shut it.

I'd be happy to. Very happy.

Good.

It's the only thing I want. To be silent.

Good.

Completely silent.

Perfect.

Not a word. Not a single letter.

[---]

Nothing. Not a single fucking sound is going to come from me.

[---]
[---]
[---]
[---]
[---]
[---]
[---]
[---]
[---]
[---]
[---]
[---]
[---]

Eh, what the fuck, man, you said you didn't have any smokes, what you lying for?

I'm not lying. You're not listening. Shit.

Fuck. It's just butts.

Yeah. I told you, bro. I told you.

[---]

You're not listening.

[---]

Shit.

That's real ghetto-talk right there. Maluch would be proud.

Maluch can go screw himself in the arse. It's his fault we got fucked. We should go and merk him.

Don't lose your shit.

No way. It was our fault too. We wanted too much.

Nothing wrong with being hungry, wanting to come up.

It was greedy. Same as with the thoughts and the words. You were right. So illogical. And now look. Two junkies hiding in a bush. Two junkies on the way to prison. I hate prison. I regret everything.

Not happening.

I hate having my freedom taken away from me. I hate sitting there with the walls and the light and my thoughts. All that stuff in your head. Thoughts and feelings. Truth and lies. And it's so quiet. I can hear myself breathing. Then I hear someone scream. Then silence again. Gives me palpitations. Must be something to do with neural networks. Something in my muscle memory. I get so stressed somehow. Scared I'm gonna lose it. That I'm gonna get sick in the head from it all, from being deprived of my freedom, from the panic and the silence, from the thoughts and the guilt and the truth going round in my head the whole time, as soon as you wake up it starts going round your head and you have to focus and focus and focus. You get crazy from it. Totally crazy. No one understands how crazy you get.

I told you. It's not happening. You need to get better at switching off, dissociating.

I regret everything, I regret my whole life.

Not happening.

No.

That's not happening.

No. It's not.

No, that's not how it happens.

[---]

[---]

Fuck it. They're coming anyway.

[---]

[---]

Now they're taking us.

[---]

[---]

Now we're gone.

Kwame

And then, as I was wandering around outside the library, looking for a key I'd lost, a man came over and started screaming at me:

'Who are you?

'Who are you?

'Do I look like a pig? Why are you following me? Do I look like a pig? Why do you hate my people? Have I fucked your mother? I'm going to kill you. Why are you following me? I'm going to kill you.

'I'm going to kill you.

'I'm going to fuck your mother.

'I'm going to kill you.

'I know your face now.

'Next time I'm going to kill you.'

Yet another name

But her name is familiar, her appearance too. Her tale is tragic and moving and makes you want to do something. Then it passes.

The weasel

So, now they're coming. Look out there. Look. They're coming. They're rolling in. The pigs. The swine. Slowly. All lined up. *Eins. Zwei. Eins. Zwei.* What do they want? What's it called? 'Carrying out official duties'. Pigs. I'll give evidence against them. What is it they're defending? Not the pigs. Their minders. Their masters and misses. Yeah. What's the word then? Mistresses. Who feed them and clear away their shit. Excrement. What's that? The people? What people? Their community behind the heat-lamps. But what kind of community is it? The cross on their flags. But there are no Christians any more. Christ is just one celeb among many. There are only apostates. The worshipping of false gods. Idols battling idols. They that have shall have more. They that don't have shall get fucked. That's it. Nation. Armed force. Economy. Armed force. Growth. Armed force. *Eins. Zwei. Polizei.* A dope car. A little bowl of mints at the bank. Massive watches and rings. And you know it's the same here as there. In the hood as in the palace. Dudes with fat wallets. As we used to say. Now you don't even need a wallet. Dudes in expensive cars. Dudes with capital and armed force. At the root of every problem you'll find a dude in an expensive car. In a plane. In a big house. With a watch that cost ninety big ones. And they call it democracy. It's like in the club. They're all: *We gon' party like it's your birthday. And you know we don't give a fuck it's not your birthday.* But fuck 'em. I'll get away from here soon. Out of this fucking place. This shitty town. This shitty country. I never asked to come here. I never asked for any of this. Fuck their respect for exile. For that experience. Screw their respect for *strong women.* They can go fuck themselves. All of 'em. *Drei. Vier. Grenadier. Fünf. Sechs. Alte Hex.*

Look. One day they'll wake up and poof. *The weasel will be gone.* She's living *la vida loca.* Like Johnny Tapia. While they're sat at home, braiding their butt hairs. What? *Was ist los? Was ist das?* Haha. I'm going to be like Tapia. A living legend. A lovely person. A real person. A junkie, sure. But a winner. And a victim too. A legend. A loser. A master. A good father and a good man. Stable and honest. But they crushed him. That's what they do with honest people. That's reality. He was a hero. Almost. Not like them. Not like the pigs out there. *Eins. Zwei.* They're still there. Dragging the kids out of their hiding places. And they love it. They're enjoying it because they love reality. We just live in it. But they love it. We fight. Because we have to. It's necessary. But they love it and they love to live in it and they love to – what's the fuckin' word? Implement. They love to implement. Yeah. Enact. Engage. Realise. Reinforce. Build it. Furnish it. The whole time with the cross on your chest. And the cross on the emblem. And the cross on the flag. I swear. Don't they know that friendship with the world means enmity towards God? To become the world's friend is to become God's enemy. That's the truth. They're the armed guards of falsehood.

What does God have to do with it? That's what they'll be grunting soon. Clueless, they are. Do you not believe that Christ was a criminal? That's the thing. The way this world is, even God becomes a terrorist. That's why we have to be averse to reality. And I mean really averse. We have to hate it. Destroy it. Be destructive. Negative. Bad. Not critical in a constructive or generous way. No. Criticism is love. We shouldn't criticise. We shouldn't give them love. We shouldn't love them. Or their reality. Which is our reality. Unfortunately. We have to hate the real people. We have to see that everything they do is about worshipping reality. Building it and strengthening it. They have the control. But they don't know it all. They think they can see what's happening by setting the limits of what can happen. They think everything is accessible. That they, and only they, have access to the truth. Of all people. And all beings. In all time and space. Only them. This fucking them. Them. Them. Them. They believe that only they have access to the truth. That it's identical to their reality. Which they're constantly constructing. That everything is that simple. And if you have any objections, they're deaf. Or they turn them to their advantage.

That's what I was saying before. Don't criticise.

But listen. The fact is, their 'implementations' just take them further away from the truth. And their hubris. Their lies. Their self-righteous shit. Their self-promotion. Everything just takes them further from what is really true. Believe me. Believe me.

Listen. You're not listening. But that's how it is. The art of listening. Tragically rare. So. All respect to those who listen.

But no one does.

Or, maybe you listen.

It's true . . . respect, all respect.

But you don't understand.

And no . . . neither do I.

Look. There they are again. The pigs. Our overlords, right?

Yeah, look, now they're dragging someone along with them. Just a body, that needs removing. Fucking pigs. But it's not their fault, I know. They're just implementing . . . something. Realising something, making something else possible.

You know, every time someone says Sweden I think about the Epistle of James.

You know:
You rich,
weep and howl
for the miseries
that are coming upon you.
Your riches have rotted
and your garments are moth-eaten.
Your gold and silver have corroded,
and their corrosion will be evidence against you
and will eat your flesh like fire.
And that is all.

Mahmoud
But at the same time, you can't ignore simple fact: the empathetically challenged child must go.

Andreas
But I started thinking about a one-time boyfriend of my mother's who used to have parties in our kitchen. It would keep my little sister awake and she'd start crying. The boyfriend would shout at her to go to bed and stop disturbing them, otherwise he'd ring the police who'd come take her away. The boyfriend used to take us for joyrides in his BMW. It was exciting; I remember how I'd get butterflies when he pushed the engine to its limit on the motorway between Malmö and Ystad. Turns out a little over a decade later he crashed his car and died on that same stretch of motorway. Party on, I thought when I heard about it.

Adela
And the funniest thing was that Grandma thought they looked shabby, but I knew that those clothes were fucking expensive and they all lived in newly renovated apartments that cost an absolute packet.

Fateful name
But to put it crudely you could say there are two kinds of people. Those for whom *ethnic cleansing* is a reality they have to come to terms with, either as a historical fact, or as personal experience, something that's directly impacted their lives, and for whom it will therefore also forever be a possibility, a potential future – and those for whom it's an abstract concept, possibly a little unpleasant, but nothing that will genuinely intrude upon their reality and alter it. That's how it is. The truth is that we all belong to the first group.

Mary
Without being able to stretch out on the bed, on work time.

Foreign names
Because while you went to view the apartment I drove down to the place under the bridge where I used to sleep sometimes in my teens

when I had nowhere to go, a place which also reminds me of S, who's homeless now too, and K, who used to suck guys off for 100 kronor in a place just like this, though in another city, in another country, and all that has always looked a little different here, in Sweden, because here everyone is valued the same, right? I mean, that's how it was, at least I think so, cos maybe it's not like that any more, now it's the same shit everywhere, more or less – that's how it feels, I don't know; there was no one there just then, but you could see someone had been sleeping there, there was even a thin foam mattress in a corner, and I wanted to lie down and have a rest, even though I knew you'd find it disgusting, because I felt so exhausted from all my thoughts, and I thought: I'm not cut out for that other stuff, I can't, I don't know how to do it, I don't have the what do you call it, the drive, or the will, or the passion, I'm lacking the tools or the motor or whatever; the fuel, or perhaps I don't want to, I'm not driven by, or how should I put it, I don't have the same motivation as you people, I don't want what you want, I just want to get away all the time, hide away, or no, that's not it, that's not really true; I don't want to be alone, for instance, I don't want to be poor, but nor do I want to collect friends like some people collect stamps or, I don't know, scout badges, or money, I don't want 'contacts', insignificant but perhaps-at-some-point-useful contacts, and I don't want my life to be governed by the fear of being poor, and there are limits to what I'll expose others to, just so I can *have a nice day*, of course I want to *have a nice day*, doesn't everyone, it's not that, it's just that I'm already *having a nice day* – (do you remember my dad, who, even when he'd learned to speak Swedish pretty well, would always mispronounce the Swedish equivalent of that phrase *have a nice day: ha det bra* – he didn't know to drop the 'r', would always say *har det bra* when he was saying bye to someone. *Hej då, har det bra!*) – it's just that I don't want to move on, up, forwards, I don't want to be bigger, better, don't want to strive, I don't know how people talk about this stuff, I just don't want to, I don't want to, I'm not able to, I have to, like, force myself to do it, and you people, yeah, what the fuck do I know, really, I know nothing about you, really, who are you, really, maybe it's the same with you, maybe you don't want to either, maybe we have to force you, maybe someone else is forcing you, maybe you're forced by all the things that got you where you are, all the things that got you what you have, maybe it's precisely that drive that enabled you to get all the things you get; or perhaps you don't want to either, perhaps there's no one who really *wants* to strive, perhaps it's just fear, they're scared of losing grip, falling, infinitely, I don't know, the fear of one day being the one who lies down to rest on a foam mattress under a bridge, looking up at the fissures and stains in the concrete – consoling themselves that in just a few short years nothing will matter, everything gets forgotten, everything fades, all meaning falls away, always – and I don't know, I really don't know, and it's good to think and say I don't know, because that's something you would never allow yourselves; but I never did lie down, I just sat for a while and smoked a few cigarettes, then went to the supermarket, and when I was there I cut myself on a piece of paper, got a paper cut by the fruit display, and I thought, as I stood there by the pomegranates and the bananas and the kiwi fruits, and saw the blood well up on my finger, that I could be hallucinating all this and that it would be good if so; perhaps that's the only way I can let go of myself, by hallucinating – letting the phantoms take over everything – splinter – be cut up into small pieces – an image here – a word there – a sound – somewhere – everything splinters – I'm trying to get it together – make a whole – futile and vain – but honestly speaking, what's the alternative – you can't keep falling apart – I'm really trying to get it together, pull it together, repair – it's just a paper cut but standing there at the till about to pay with blood on my hand I feel like a junkie – I say nothing – I punch in my code and think how white the light is here with the black conveyor belt running past me and back, I rarely think about how it rolls past me and then under the till and back and rolls past me again and again and again – but I say nothing – and I look up and meet the cashier's uncertain gaze, her makeup, mascara, kohl pencil, brown eyes, like mine, maybe filler in her cheeks, in her lips – I say nothing – I hold my hand up, stiffly, to stop it dripping, I try to smile to reassure her, but I don't know if I succeed and I think: *just imagine if it was possible to buy guns over the counter.* And then I disappeared. I know it surprised everyone, you most of all. We had totally different plans. But I have no good explanation, I was surprised too, it surprised me that I didn't even know what the apartment was selling for, whether you could buy it. The following days were like a hole. I know it's a terrible image, really lazy, but I don't know how to describe it – and that's part of it, the not knowing – and I don't even know if a *good image* would be preferable – not even that – and not even this: the complaint, the lamentation – not even the sorrow and the hole and the emptiness – not even that – all that is pure – it's yours – I'm something else, something impure in your world – there's nothing strange about it, they used to say, even in my teens – it's post-traumatic life – there's nothing strange about it – nothing wrong with you really – it's a natural reaction – you have to realise for yourself that all natural things are good – but I don't know – and perhaps I don't want to know – it's not that I lack the words – the words exist – far too many words exist – it's not that – I don't want them – I want to get away from them – get away from myself, in them – I wish I didn't exist, that only you existed – in some other way, but that's impossible, it sounds strange and unfeasible – I know – anyway – I don't know – I took my telephone and computers and put them in the bath tub, then filled it with water. A few days passed, my finger stopped bleeding, I went to the supermarket again, the cashier wished me a nice day and I returned the gesture, a little mechanically maybe, but it was honestly meant, and everything was back to normal. In some ways. A ninety-year-old woman had been robbed. Two police officers were asking her questions about the incident. I got the sense they didn't believe her. A beggar on the street outside the shop. Another, twenty metres along, of another kind: walking, 'Swedish'. New Year's Eve was approaching. I bought some cheap Portuguese wine, onions, tomatoes, parmesan, yogurt for breakfast. I thought about how everything was going to get worse, harder, harsher. That it's better that way, fairer. I thought: 2020 is a pre-war time. There's something not quite right. Failing defence mechanisms. I'm sad. The pre-war time is nearly over. It's true. It was a good time. It was the end of the twentieth century, extended. That mustn't be right, it can't be right. No one saw it coming. Not even people staring hard into the future with their money and high-tech cameras. 2020 was a good year. As sharp and heavy as an axe. I thought, when it comes down to it, I'm an impressively imaginative person, just like everyone else, bound-lessly inspired, apparently, even when it comes to stupidity and foolishness. I prepare my answers to your questions. Soon I'm going to decide whether to carry on like this or go back to your life. I think about it every day, because I wrote a note that I keep on the kitchen table, that says: MAKE UP YUR MIND! GET IN TOUCH! I was tired, so I spelled the word *your* wrong. On the back it says: ME / 2020 / BEFORE THE WAR.

Muslim name
And everything rhymes.

D
And here's the story behind the video: we're driving up Gullregnsvägen and we notice there's a fight so I get my phone out and start filming, and I tell D to slow down and then we see a guy and two women kicking the shit out of one of the cleaners from school; his trolley is on the ground, and D drives up and winds down the window and one of the people laying into him says *Rapist, he raped a girl* and D says *Is he a rapist?* The guy's trying to protect himself from the kicks and blows and D stops the car and says *Wait, wait, I want in on this*, and then he jumps out of the car like before it's even stopped

fully, and I'm just filming the whole time, and D kind of jogs over to the guy, the rapist, who's there on the grass, kneeling with one hand on the ground and the other in front of his face to protect himself, and D gives him a smack in the face so he topples over and then one of the girls comes up and stamps three or four times on his back, but he gets up and gets another massive smack in the face from D and it carries on until D seems to think *Enough, the cops'll be here soon* or maybe: *But what if he's innocent*, and he jumps back into the car and yeah, that's when I stop filming.

Important name
Because every time I betray someone or hit someone or hurt someone in some other way, I will draw attention to my name; my name is everything to me, my beginning and my end, my form and my function, my contours and my depth, my mirror and my loneliness, my all.

Jessica
But no, I'm not sure. Of course they were proud and everything. But not totally – how can I put it – unreservedly. I mean, maybe they felt a bit like they'd been steamrollered. And I got shit for teaching them a lesson. Or like they thought I was coming in, thinking I knew it all. How everything was, and how it should be. Just because I'd got an education. And they thought I looked down on them. Or that they were worse, worth less than me. But I didn't. Yeah, yeah, they said. You know it all, right? You know it all. But I never got into that discussion. Because it was so obvious it was all rooted in their low self-esteem. But I would never, ever look down on them. Never. At least not because they didn't know this or that, or because they didn't understand a particular, I don't know, analysis or abstraction, or a particular historical, I don't know, set of circumstances, I don't know, or that they hadn't heard of particular facts or names or dates or whatever, or that their relationship to knowledge was, how can I put it, I don't know, pragmatic, or – no, how should I put it?

Changed name

That is, the faint scent of urine when I put my mouth to their genitals.

Slávik

But then I was suddenly forced to move out of my house in just a few hours. My wife, my children, all of us had to get out, because they were going to tear it down or renovate it or whatever, it wasn't clear exactly what was going to happen, and the thing is that we had nowhere to go, no other house, or apartment, or set-up, so we ran around, looking for a suitably clean place to leave our stuff until we could sort all this out, this whole 'living situation' — I remember this phrase filling me with panic, it was as though every time I or someone else used it I slipped a little further away from myself, as though I was my own lifebuoy somehow and every time I, or someone else, said 'living situation', a wave came and like, swept away the lifebuoy a little, and then someone said 'living situation' — a little further — 'living situation' — and a little further, but it was raining, and everywhere was dirty, or full of people casting weird, or evil, or covetous, or simply eccentric looks at us, so we couldn't find anywhere, and the time passed, and soon I had to leave because my shift was starting, and my wife said she'd sort us somewhere to live, and my kids said they'd look after the stuff, and they told me not to worry, everything will work out, everything will be alright, Dad — and I started to panic, because those were my responses — and they smiled and hugged me, and I left my wife and my kids and took the car, it was dark, and for some reason all the cars I met kept driving over onto my side of the road, so I had to keep swerving the whole time to avoid crashing, and then I got to work, it was me and two Poles, then we loaded things into a truck (it's like Tetris, but kind of horizontal, I was thinking, to console myself), they were things Siavosh, the boss, had bought cheap somewhere and was going to sell for a high price, or at least higher.

Buy low, sell high, guys, he said to us in English, even though we all spoke Swedish, the key to success, guys, remember: buy low, sell high. Buy low, sell high.

But soon it was midnight, the deadline had passed and I didn't know how things had worked out for my wife and kids – they were going to have to carry all the stuff down, they were going to be forced to move out with nowhere to move to, so I was going to ask Siavosh if I could leave, but he took off without replying, so I just stood there a while, blinking awkwardly in the rain, but then I pulled myself together and said to Maciek: I'm going now, try to cover if you can, tell him . . . I don't know . . . make something up, but don't exaggerate, it has to be believable, nothing unrealistic or totally wild, and Maciek said: OK, just to calibrate, is James Bond unrealistic in your eyes? You think the Bible is wild? But then I said I didn't have time for splitting hairs, my kids are on the street, and he said, slightly disappointed, that's OK, semantics and splitting hairs aren't really the same thing, but I get that you're in a tight spot right now, it's cool, he said, of course, I'll sort it. But there's a problem: my phone's broken, lost all my numbers, give me your number so I can ring you on the landline if shit goes down, and I said OK, and I was going to write it on his hand, but first of all the pen didn't work, and then when I did write it I wrote from my side, on his right hand, but then he said he couldn't read it that way so I said OK, give me your left hand, but then his whole arm uncoiled, like a snake or something, and I couldn't write on his skin because he was sweaty and the dust had stuck to his sweat, the dust from the floor of the truck and the stuff Siavosh was going to *sell high*, so I got my knife and started scraping to get at his skin, and then I was like, whittling away at his arm, like, slicing off these great wood-like flakes, and Maciek was crying out from the pain but laughing too and he said: What is this? Am I Pinocchio or what? And even though I was scared and horribly stressed I couldn't help laughing too, and I said that's what happens if you lie to the boss, and Maciek said he hadn't even got to the lying bit yet, what are you, a time-traveller? And we were crying with laughter, we were crying and we just stood there a good while, saying *Jesus Christ, Jesus Christ, Jesus Christ*, but in the end we decided I could carve my number into this wood-like flesh, but I had a better idea and got a soldering iron and burned it in instead, and then, when I got home, our landlord was there eating an ice cream he'd made himself, it was basil flavoured, he said, adding that it was more *gelato* than ice cream, because it was made with milk, breast milk, if you know what I mean, he said with a grin, it takes a very long time to make. When I didn't respond, he grew serious and asked me if I really believed it was true, that he bought, or even maybe took, stole, obtained by force, women's breast milk. I'm assuming you know it's in short supply on neonatal units around the country, they pay between 100 and 200 kronor for a litre, so I have to cough up even more. You think I'm lying, exaggerating, or do you believe it's true? What do you think? And then he said: Listen, I'm going to explain something to you. One of the hardest things in the world is *to not hate those who have* when you yourself *have not*. But . . . and this is important . . . it's just as hard to not *hate yourself* when you *have* what others *don't have*. You see where I'm going with this? I can't . . . I can never, never, *never* . . . allow you to minimise *my* suffering. You see? Do you understand what I'm saying? Are you capable of taking that in? That *I too* am suffering.

Dagmar
And that a thousand wolves would come and take me if I didn't do the right thing.

Ligaya
That is to say Ligaya, who collected cans and wiped the bins clean. No one had asked her to do it. The rounded, sloped surface that people snubbed out cigarettes and spat on. Filthy, stinking Ligaya. Psycho-Ligaya who always held your gaze. Mama Ligaya who'd once hired her six-year-old son out to four men for eight hours and then

coldly defended herself by saying the side effects of the meds had made her confused. But that was many years ago. An indescribable time that had suddenly come to an end. Now her son was gone, and the men too. Now 'correctional healthcare' was nothing but an old joke, just one more thing to prove that nothing would ever break her. The staff in the smoking shelter outside the addiction centre recognised her and said *Hi Ligaya, kumusta Ligaya?* They were friendly and warm and generous. Beautiful, gentle, vanilla girls. Ligaya answered *Hi, thank you, thank you so much.* And then they turned away and she turned away and she lifted her filth-laden woollen coat and whispered into her warm armpit curses and expletives so coarse and brutal she could feel the shame and the excitement making her heart pound, and she felt the blood pulsing around her body, coursing through her veins, in her temples, her throat, her heart and down into her cunt which grew heavy and moist and she felt herself growing stronger and stronger with every day that passed.

Miki
Because it feels so far away now, that Dad did all those things . . . I can't even remember what any more.

Many names
Or what difference does it make anyway? Someone says your name. Or someone asks you what your name is. Or someone pronounces your name wrong. Or someone can't be bothered to say your name. Or someone says the wrong name altogether. Or someone gives you a new name you love. Or one you don't like. Or someone has the same name as you, and you become reflections of each other.

Anders (temporary sales name)
Or when it comes to hijinks and that – yeah, I've never told anyone this, but yeah, when I was like sixteen, seventeen there was this sick thing we used to do. Or, not used to do, but yeah, we did it a few

times. We got the idea after Lajos's brother showed us these two films. He was one of those guys who was in adult education and he knew about a load of weird stuff. So he showed us these two films, *A Clockwork Orange* and *Funny Games*, they were called. In both films there are these guys who take people hostage in their own homes. And us lot, we'd done a few minor smash-and-grab bits, like corner shops and stuff, mostly for the fun of it to be honest, I mean for the kick, maybe for smokes a couple of times, or pocket money. But now we thought we'd go up a level. So we'd go out to those massive houses down by the sea when it was dark, you know, where Zlatan had a house later on. We'd find a spot to leave our mopeds and track down a house where the family were at home. We'd check pretty carefully to see whether they had dogs but otherwise we weren't fussed, whether there were kids or not, whether there were old people, all those sorts of things. We'd put our masks on or those balaclavas, you know, and we'd climb over the fence. Then we'd storm the place, in through the doors, the windows, whatever. When we got inside we'd run around, shouting and smashing shit up. We never took anything and we never touched the people inside. Mostly they were completely paralysed, probably from like shock or whatever. We'd go crazy for a few minutes, six or seven minutes max, no longer, that was enough, then it was over; we had a code word we'd shout, I can't remember what it was exactly, it was from one of those films, a Russian word I think. Then we'd run back to the mopeds and all drive off in different directions. The feeling was totally mind-blowing, like some incredible drug. It was like your whole body was humming, electric, and as long as you were with the others you didn't feel any regret or anything either. It was only later, when you were on your own, that the anxiety might kick in, especially if there'd been kids there, or, like, if you'd taken their fear into yourself, I mean if you'd acknowledged them somehow, I don't know how to explain it. But that passed sooner or later. And then one time — it was the last time — this horrible thing happened. At that time I was doing a bit of extra work with my brother, some cash-in-hand stuff – legal – like on building sites, removals, cleaning, chauffeuring, whatever. So one day he rang and said he had a cleaning job and needed an extra pair of hands. I said OK, no questions asked, and he came and picked me up a few days later. We're sitting in the car and he starts driving towards the sea. I get a weird feeling so I start asking him about the job. And then he tells me one of his boss's colleagues or something had a break-in at home and a load of stuff was destroyed and we were going to be the ones clearing it up. As soon as he said that stuff I knew, somehow, that it was going to be the same house we'd been in. Catastrophe. I died, I swear. But anyway, we head over, and of course it's the same place. The family aren't there, they've gone away or are staying with relatives or whatever. But some man was walking around, I think he was a caretaker or something, he was the one who'd hired us. And he was walking around, moaning the whole time: *Why? Why? How could anyone do something like this, totally meaningless, it's not even about the money. Why? Why? Why?* And we're cleaning and cleaning, and I'm getting more and more annoyed with him, and simultaneously more and more scared. I can't explain it. I wasn't scared of getting banged up, I don't think, but I felt hounded somehow, I don't know how to describe it. I didn't want to be alone, but I also didn't want my brother to notice anything, so the whole time I was keeping an eye on where he was. And suddenly, as I was filling a plastic bucket with like a hundred or maybe a thousand little shards of glass, I started seeing things, as though something was moving, although there was nothing there, like there was this fluttering in front of my face, and I thought this must be some kind of revenge, it wasn't normal, it was a threat, the pigs that lived there had done something to my brain. And here was this guy, going around with his *why, why* and I thought, something's about to happen, something really bad is about to happen, and I started imagining how I'd walk past a mirror and there'd be nothing there, I mean like I'd have no reflection, or that my brother and this caretaker would take revenge on me, that there was some big cop living here and he had contacts and knew everything and was going to torture us in the garage with the tools that were hanging there, all in perfect order. My heart was pounding and I was sweating abnormally. Yeah, I was flipping out to be honest. But then it passed. I went to the toilet and washed my face. I saw my reflection, I saw how it turned its face away when I turned mine. So everything was normal. Then I had a smoke and went on cleaning, listening to the caretaker guy and his meaningless questions.

Gesche
For she arose as you entered the parlour. With faint displeasure, she experienced the way your eyes caressed her as she made her exit.

Without name
But I know there's a hidden, secret life beneath the life that is freely accessible. The real one, the important one. At night it is images, memories of the future, without words. In the day it comes as waves of language, of sounds that can't be heard, of voices without bodies. I'm a simple person and I want to live a simple life. Clear and real. But it's hard. There are demons. I can't describe them because they shape-shift. They're animals, children, relatives, friends, reflections. Furniture, even; objects. Trees and plants. Electronics intensify their essence. The world is big and my life, the sum of my sensory experience, is insignificant. I walk through a forest of apple trees, someone must have planted them. I remember when I helped a friend prune some apple trees a few years back. It was autumn. An arborist had shown us how to do it. I stood on a rusty ladder, everything was soaking wet. The trees were like animals. The bark was like skin. They were old trees, at least sixty years old, and we tried to picture what the root system might look like. Apparently the arborist had said that most roots don't grow deeper than twenty or so centimetres beneath the ground. That image of the roots as a reflection of the tree's crown is a misconception, she said. I come to a house; it looks deserted. I go

into the kitchen. Make tea, eat a few crackers. I'm alone but it feels like there's someone here with me. As though someone is watching me, judging me. I feel unjustly treated, but also calm. The house asks my name. I have no answer.

Bella and Taimur

Because the money was running dry, our rent went up, the benefits office were on my back. The children wanted toys and I wanted them to have clean, practical clothes. So I applied for a job and went to the interview in Landskrona. I was half an hour early for the interview, so I went into a café to get a coffee. It was a small room with space for four or five tables. There were three teenagers sitting at one of them, two girls and a guy. The guy was tall and looked like a regular Swedish-blonde-hair-blue-eyes type. One of the girls, who seemed to be called Bella, was working some kind of white-trash style, and the other, who appeared to be dating the blonde guy, looked kind of Romani and had extremely long nails she kept staring at. Bella was talking, the blonde guy was looking from her to his phone. I can't exactly reproduce the way she said this, but it was something like: 'Taimur's so cute, you know. He says I'm his guardian angel. And it's true 'n all. He told me when I called him the first time he was standing by the tracks and was about to jump. We'd only met once, you know, and I took his number but it took a while, cos I was busy with my course and stuff, but then I was thinking about him and I called. And at that very moment he was down by the tracks, planning to kill himself. He was doing really badly. A lot of his friends had got sent back and one had already taken his own life. And that's when I called. And it made him so happy he decided not to jump when the train came. And then we got together. I really am his guardian angel.'

I drank the rest of my coffee and went to the interview, where a passive-aggressive head teacher asked a couple of questions before diving deep into this cliché-laden monologue about how we were living in a new era, that social media would soon replace books, that he himself preferred to look recipes up online rather than in some sauce-splattered old cookbook. The phone is the new book, he said. After ten minutes I could no longer hear what he was saying. I looked out the window. The trees looked black against the pale grey sky. I thought of the guardian angel Bella's story and tried to picture Taimur, by the tracks, with a book, a book that spoke to him, that persuaded him not to jump.

Frasse
'Although, at the same time, it's becoming clearer and clearer what the whole point of this memory work is,' he said. 'We remember the oppression of the past so we don't have to deal with the consequences of the oppression that's currently happening. Right now I'm thinking about putting some staples into my forearm. Three rows, all the way from my wrist to my elbow. That's a memory. The mornings were fantastic, *insanely* good coffee and the scent of freshly baked bread, watermelon, black olives and a white, creamy, mild cheese. Another memory. Then the gathering went on all day until the sun went down. There were twelve of us: three Europeans, a Ghanaian, four Chileans and a control team from Azerbaijan, there were four of them. I lost all my luggage and spent several hours searching for it in the station. Nothing seemed to mean anything until I'd found it again. Sorry. I wish apparently insignificant things also had meaning. Especially for me, since I'm never going to meet another human being again. I've become one of those people. "Nameless", "marginalised", pure nonsense. In my defence, all I can say is that this is what I thought you had to do to succeed in the world you inhabit. You have to erase yourself or perish, you have to adapt and silence yourself or perish, you have to give up the struggle or perish. It's always rawer and more brutal than we can imagine. I want them to understand something,' he said. 'The class system is a very, very, very violent place, irrespective of where in the hierarchy you find yourself. It's dark, it's night.

Someone's drawing, sketching souls and Goya's painting of Saturn eating his own children. The eyes. My namesake.'

Hidden name

But she consoled herself with the fact that most of them have no idea how to clean, and so they flush the toilet with the lid open, which means the contents − tiny, tiny particles, but still, her shit and piss − splash two metres up, onto their clean clothes and their clean faces and into their clean mouths and nostrils and then deep into their lungs.

Fitting name

But at the time I was a teacher. I guess I was nineteen or twenty. Unqualified, of course. The kids were in secondary school. I would get out a load of instruments . . . you know . . . drums, tambourines, guitars, there was a piano, a synth, a melodica, and so on . . . and then I'd have them pick a piece of paper with a word on it. They were mostly adjectives describing different kinds of feelings: angry, sad, lonely, hungry. And happy. So they got a piece of paper and they had to test out the instruments and finally try to like . . . play the words. Then I got them to listen to some music, different kinds of music that I'd chosen . . . quite short excerpts, classical composers, drum & bass, hip hop, death metal, you know, all sorts. And the kids were meant to sit there and write down associations, single words, whatever, words they started thinking of when they heard the music. And . . . there were a few who . . . wrote things like, 'I'm thinking about the time when . . . the soldiers came and . . . took my uncle . . . and they shot him later' . . . and then a picture, it was a picture of some bodies that had sort of been thrown down on the ground in a forest clearing. You know . . . like . . . well . . . And I realised that these kids had seen . . . had experienced . . . And I couldn't handle it. I didn't say anything to them and I didn't say anything to the other teachers because I knew there were no resources for dealing with

these kinds of things. I mean, the kids' experiences. Although I . . .
yeah, what did I do? I went home and cried. And then later I handed
in my notice. Got a new job. The kids drew pictures for me. *We'll
miss you*, and so on . . . it felt like I'd let them down . . . and myself, to
be honest. But I don't know. When I was little there was a guy who
lived in my building. He used to boast how he'd been a soldier in
his home country. That he'd killed people with a bayonet and things
like that. A lot of sick things, he told us. Everyone believed him, us
kids I mean. Since then I've thought it couldn't have been true, of
course. These days I don't know what to believe. Because these days
I know absolutely anything can be true.

Name that means ruler
And that's how it is. I really go mad every time I have to do the
vacuuming at home. It's true. At work, that's one thing, but at home,
I can't. That's how it is.

Your name and mine
And sometimes we get to have the same name. But listen, my parents
clean your parents' offices and your parents' big houses. You and
I – we're not the same.

Barbro and Elias
So now I'm going to try and be clear. Clear as crystal. Or . . . rain-
drops. Drip, drip, drip. Yes, well. And I can get a little muddled,
when no one's listening. Or silent for several days – yes, it's true;
for several weeks . . . Perhaps before the fog lifts I'll even pass away,
to use that rather delicate phrase. But yes, well . . . I used to be able
to talk non-stop. Hour after hour. I didn't need to think. Talking was
meaningful then. That's the way it felt, anyway. A person like me,
the way I was, I just reacted to the world around me. If I opened my
mouth, words and sentences simply came out. Nag, nag. Then I realised nothing mattered. That . . . one was insignificant. Or . . . well . . .

that no one paid any attention to what you said, they just heard what they wanted to hear – I mean, that's how it was. And you were to be quiet. They heard alright, but it made no difference. I used to say to Haris that he shouldn't drive so much, that he shouldn't smoke such an awful lot, and never more than two large shots an hour, or three beers. He always fobbed me off. But I guess I was right in the end. Yes, but it made no difference. You can't say *I told you so* to a grave. You just can't. That's not how it works.

And then there's the dog. What was the matter with it? Never listened. Bit one of our children, that dog did. Yes, there were no lasting . . . injuries, or anything, but it drew blood, to be sure. So we put it down. Laika, its name was, after that space dog, yes, or well, Haris put it down. Hit it on the head in the garage, I think, back then you did that kind of thing yourself. There was nothing odd about it. Then we buried her down by the river. It had to be done, sure, but we were still sad, the children in particular. But if you bite, you'll get what's coming to you. Maybe they'll do the same to me soon. If I bite someone. There are several people I'd like to bite. I could get my teeth sharpened, what do you reckon, then I guess they would draw blood, I guess they would, though my jaws aren't so strong these days, perhaps because I so rarely say anything, and I don't do a lot of chewing either, I don't eat much, I mean most things are pretty soft, no. Just split peas and that kind of thing, mostly, or yes, I can't ever remember what we have, there's meat too, yes there is, actually, pig I think it is mostly, pork, if they sort of mash the cutlet in some way after it's been fried, it's dry, dry meat, you see. Very dry, even if it's been mashed. I tend to take a little milk out of my glass with a spoon and sort of moisten the meat after they've mashed it for me, that's what I do, and it becomes even more like mash. Yes. Would they put me down? If I started biting? Is that a strange thing to say? Out to the garage and bang.

Laika . . . later we found out what really happened to the space dog. Well, it died of fright after just a few hours . . . died of fright after a few hours, yes, and orbited the earth several thousand times before burning up, apparently. But we didn't know that, we had no idea, both Haris and I were fans of the Soviet Union at that time, and all that Sputnik stuff was new. Sputnik 2, yes, or was it Sputnik 3? And the dog had to have a name. Laika sounded lovely. In the pictures it was so sweet and happy and brave, somehow, I guess everyone thought that, we didn't know it had already died of fright, after just a few hours. This didn't come out until much, much later, it was just a few years ago – ten or twelve years ago. I suppose I was about eighty then. I'll be ninety-two soon, it's madness . . . Or am I already ninety-two . . . Elias is only ninety. But yes, I remember when I heard it on the radio, I was sitting over there, over by the window, I think it was winter, snow in the yard, on the trees, suet balls, songbirds, nice and calm, that was before the pain, and someone turned on the radio – I don't tend to listen to the radio myself, it doesn't give me anything any more, it mostly feels like I'm eavesdropping, as though those voices are talking to someone else and I've just got in the way, it's as though nothing has anything to do with me, you see – but anyway, there I was, sitting quietly, and someone put the radio on. And they were talking about space I think, or about animals, about animal testing, perhaps, animal rights, and how we shouldn't abuse pigs and whales and so on, and then they said that Laika had died of fright after just a few hours, and I thought it was so awful. It didn't at all fit with the image I had of the whole business. Of what had happened back then. We wouldn't have called the puppy Laika if we'd known all that. It sounds awful, but that's how it is. Yes, life's like that. And here I am, ninety-two years old, and I've not died of fright yet.

But our Lord is with us . . . out there.

Isn't that right, Elias dear?

I said: The Lord is with us!

No.

He can't hear.

Yet another forgotten name
For the rich, she said, will stay rich, and the poor will stay violent. That much we can rely on.

X
And the worst thing is this feeling that not a single minute is spent doing something for my own sake, not a single second. Everything I do, I do for someone else, or on behalf of someone else, or to someone else. The whole time I have someone else in my line of sight, in my sight, in my dreams; this is it, this is the thing, the worst thing, that I'm hounded all the time, I can never just relax and enjoy myself, just enjoy life. That's the thing.

Immigrant name
But when I said I don't eat eggs, she almost lost it completely, this person, she got, like, hysterical, and said, like, you don't eat eggs because you feel sorry for the animals, but you buy clothes here, and here, and you do this and that with no thought for all the people who wear themselves to the bone so you can have this and that, and the drugs, yeah the drugs, are they organic? Are they fair trade drugs, eh? Are they really all ethically certified? And so on and in the end it got totally wild.

Turpal
And when Turpal died, his daughter went through his desk and found a black notebook with the words *Brepols / Back to paper / Notes*. She sat down right there on the rickety white chair – which he'd sat on since the early nineties, thousands of hours, hundreds of evenings, nights and mornings – and she slowly deciphered the Cyrillic letters, phoneme by phoneme, morpheme by morpheme. Somewhere, vague and distant, she could sense her father's words, his images, his secret life, but the gaps were too many and she soon gave up. A few days later, she made a second attempt, with a computer and an old Soviet dictionary to hand:

God's light. Only trust people who are conscious of their own absolute insignificance. God's light.

God's light. Everyone else will stab you in the back. They want to see you on your knees. They're using you. They'll sell you, first chance they get. They'll forget you. They're laughing at you when you're not around to see. They'll never see you. They see what they want to see, which means they are blind. God's light.

God's light. Tonight I'll clean the Swedes' offices. The corridors, waiting rooms, toilets. This clean people. What I experience at that moment, in a captive, encapsulated light, is a struggle with the world, and it's a struggle with myself. God's light.

God's light. All these *whys*. Why? Why? God's light.

God. Why must we always struggle and suffer? When will it end? God, I ask you, why am I not dead? Why didn't I die by that bus stop outside Vladikavkaz with Emin — when his blood dried on my hand and I howled like a dog <u>Don't die, Don't die</u> and <u>Take me instead, take me. God, take me instead.</u>

God, why didn't you take me instead, why won't you take me now?

God's light. Blind. I'm blind to that which shows itself in silence, in composure. Blind and mute. Who will drive away the words and images as the matter, the objects, the circumstances drove us away? God, forgive me this quasi-Marxism, but what is it that has made me half a person, mute, deaf, maimed? Blind and forced to see it. Blind. I am blind. But I can see. God's light.

God's light. Nothing happens, nothing can happen. The whole afternoon is instead sunk in some reverie. The whole afternoon is sunk in something numinous. A dignity that does not exist here. A wisdom. I am sure. I believe. I hope. A peaceful anticipation of that final peace. God's light.

MY CHILDREN ARE SLIPPING FROM MY HANDS · THEY WILL NEVER RETURN · THEY CANNOT REMEMBER WHAT I HAVE FORGOTTEN · THEY ARE BLIND AS I AM BLIND · BLIND BLIND BLIND · I AM BLIND BLIND BLIND · I AM BLIND · I AM BLIND BLIND BLIND · EVERYTHING IS SLIPPING FROM MY HANDS · I AM BLIND · I AM BLIND BLIND BLIND · MY HANDS ARE MOVING · I AM BLIND · I AM BLIND BLIND BLIND · I WASH MY HANDS OF IT · BLIND · FOR WHOM AM I WASHING MY HANDS · MY CHILDREN

Dino
But I'm going to win. Everything.

Jörg/Yuri
And the feel of designer clothes, you know.

Maggan
Or like those spirals, that it goes round and round and round.

No name
Because we have no past, no language. Relief and gratitude. Thank you so much. It's fine, that's just fine. No future, no time at all. A choir is singing *Dona nobis pacem*, and at the same time, somewhere else, the war goes on.

Christian name
And I haven't done anything today.

Assumed name
Or for instance, the guy at the nudist pool who was flexing his muscles.

Tadeusz
But what were we doing at the construction site? Cleaning. Going around in our work clothes, like a uniform, feeling a sense of belonging, that there was some meaning to our existence. I don't know what else you want to hear about it . . .

Victoria
Or the fact that deep down I agree that that kind of violence can be seen as self-inflicted social cleansing, even if I wouldn't put it in those terms. Not publicly.

NN
Apart from the fact it was also much too warm.

Two children's names
Like, absolutely everything, then. Absolutely everything. Smashing windows . . . kicking in lockers . . .
    Yeah, and lights, we smashed those . . . kicked them to pieces. And punctured the tyres on bikes, mopeds and cars.
    Blew up postboxes. And electricity units.
    We set fire to bins too. Skips. Graffiti.
    Slashed seats and sofas. Cut them up.
    And clothes too. In the shops and, what are they called? Cloakrooms.
    Shoved stuff in exhaust pipes. Potatoes and that.
    And in the petrol tanks, sugar, sand, but nothing happened.
    No. But the thing with the lifts . . .
    Oh yeah. Surfing the lifts.
    Yeah.
    You open the lift door, get a cable and put it up where the door closes and then you can press the buttons, even though the doors are open. Then it goes down and you can stand on top of it.
    Yeah, you kind of ride on the top. Put a load of stuff up there. Or like, undo a screw.

Or just ride it. Surf.

Yeah, you could steer it from up there. Up and down. Up and down. Then that thing with the shots.

Yeah, someone had found some bullets, and then we put them on the May Day bonfire, like before they lit it.

Waited and waited, but nothing happened.

Nothing.

Then a load of small shit. Staples on chairs. And spitting in the food.

That laxative stuff in the squash.

Yeah, and one time a bit of hash in the teacher's coffee. Or washing-up liquid, normally.

Glue in the locks. Yeah, there was a lot of things. To be honest.

Yeah. Putting viruses on the school computers. Cutting wires.

Yeah, the wires. We cut them.

What else. Nicking stuff. Everywhere. All sorts . . . at school, shops, break-ins, cars, everything.

Yeah, and . . . chewing gum, you know. And glue in the locks. Or, uh, I said that. But cutting wires?

Yeah. Setting off the fire alarm. Burning cars and mopeds.

And bike sheds.

Yeah.

Pushed a car in the canal too.

Threw stones at the police. At fire engines. Even ambulances.

And buses. And shining lasers, shooting air guns or BB guns.

And catapults, and those kinds of tubes with a balloon on one end.

And spraying pepper spray in the hall, just as everyone was coming out.

Loosening nuts – what's the word – screws, on bikes and that.

Piercing holes in condoms. Shit like that.

Yeah. I don't know . . . what else.

I don't know. I'm sure there was something.

Yeah, absolutely everything.

Actual name

Because he used to clean the record shop too. But they would never let him touch the records (even though he'd once shared a stage with Dexter Gordon (Copenhagen 1973) whose LP was on sale there for €75 (half a week's wages for him)).

A name

And the man with the white hat, white clothes and a white scooter who shouts, 'It belongs to me!' when the metro comes in. 'This is my train!' Two minutes later he's singing 'Silent Night' and crying, 'Mama! Mama!' before he gets a punch in the face from a young smack addict who thinks the singing and the shouting are ruining his begging.

A name

Because soon the parents will be drunk.

A name

And that everyone has to have someone beneath them.

A name

Or that exercise with everything on the breakfast table. Every single thing. The butter knife, the bread, the bread wrapper, the breadbasket, the muesli, the turkey slices, the tomatoes, the eggs, the spoons, the salt cellar. And so on. Where do they come from? Imagine every act of labour that was required to get them to your breakfast table. Who manufactured them, shipped them, sold them? Who made the most money from them? And so on. Every morning, every morning. The repetition, the rattle. Like a psycho.

A name

And the alcohol sweats. My sister and I used to joke about how we always thought of Dad when we went into certain shops, because of that special bottle deposit machine smell. Or magic markers, you know? And that's to say nothing of the ambivalent appeal of our own intoxication, those immediate, cosy sensations of frictionlessness and relief.

Too many names
And today I couldn't work because I couldn't stop thinking about the shooting. It was all too raw.

New Swedish name
But it's just a name. What does it matter?

A name
And everything you do is advertising for something.

A name
Or that I like that thing where stuff tastes of plastic, half-poisonous, I feel at home in the scent of coal and coke from stoves and boilers in those rental places. That I feel at home in that impoverished country.

A name
Because everything will one day come tumbling down. Even the climbers, the wannabes, the men and women in the corridors, behind the desks, in the conference centres, the taxis, at the spa hotels, in the lifts, on the way up, up to their downfall.

Daniil
And that's actually all.

No name
And nothing.

The last name

So after that I stopped painting completely. Yes, it was almost twenty years ago now. But I still don't know if I can say what I wanted to 'get across' with those paintings, the last ones. 'Get across', it sounds like . . . in a debate, you know. I don't know, it was more that I wanted to project something. Bring it into the light, without really knowing what we should do with it. I guess I thought that if I have an image in my head, so to speak, within me, then I should share it, regardless of what that image is.

So the first one was of a suicide in London, in the eighteenth century. A man – a poor man with a big family – made it known, far and wide, that he was planning to commit suicide in public, on a stage, so to speak, as long as enough people paid him a small sum, that is, bought tickets. The money would go to the widow and children. The story, as I've encountered it, doesn't reveal whether the performance took place or not. But I saw them before me, the children, at a table, as they ate the food their mother had bought with the money. The hunger that was sated. Yeah. And that was it. Some children eating food. It's a simple scene.

And the other was a hanging, in the same city, a little over a hundred years later. A man slit his throat, but his life was saved by a doctor who managed to sew his throat back together. Trying to commit suicide was punishable by death, so it was soon decided that he'd be hanged. The doctors warned: the wound hasn't healed, his throat will open up, but nobody listened. The man was hanged, the wound opened up and he was able to breathe again. Then a scene took place that Nikolay Ogarev depicted in a letter to Mary Sutherland, the girl he helped get out of the slums and prostitution of the West End, in 1859: 'At length the aldermen assembled and bound up the neck below the wound *until he died*. O my Mary, what a crazy society and what a stupid civilization.' I saw that circle of aldermen, with the condemned suicide victim in the background. Their bodies, the very figures of power, and – yeah – that idiocy dressed up as common sense and logic.

And then the third, really the central painting, which was to be flanked by the aforementioned two. It was a complicated story, which I heard somewhere, and which immediately brought to mind Ilya Repin's portrait of Ivan the Terrible and his murdered son. You know, he's sitting there, with the bloody head in his arms. A panicked, wild-eyed look, the terror of the tyrant when he catches a glimpse of himself. This story, which took place somewhere in western Europe, post-war, was about a man who'd lived a hard life. He grew up poor, turned to crime early, got into drugs, was violent and so on. He met a woman, they married, had a son, and this last thing in particular was an experience that seemed to change him deeply, to soften him. But sadly, before the transformation was complete, or however you put it, he got into a situation where, under pressure, he found it necessary to turn to violence, which resulted in his opponent, his enemy in that moment, losing his life. He was caught and convicted of murder. After a while, his wife left him, they divorced and he lost contact with his son. Then . . . many years later, with just a few years until his release, he wrote a letter to his son, in the hope of, if not resuming contact, at least getting to meet him when he came out. He wrote a long, emotional, open-hearted letter to his son, where he talked of his life and his hopes for the future. He begged for forgiveness and asked for a meeting. He sent it off and waited for a response. Weeks passed, no reply. Months, no reply. He sat down a second time, wrote a new letter, this time including a number of anecdotes he'd written down while in prison, more or less dramatic experiences he believed had made him into the person he was. 'I'm not an evil man,' he wrote. 'But I've had a lot of evil around me. And on occasion it has also forced its way inside me.' Then he posted that letter too. And waited. And waited. No reply . . . So the years pass. And then he comes out. Only a few days after his release he meets his son. It turns out that he, now a successful writer, has written a novel based on the man's letters, on his father's life. His son gives him a copy, and he reads a few pages while the son goes to get them some wine, but he soon puts the book down, terrified. They spend the evening together. He stays the night. His son falls asleep. He starts to read the book again, can't stop himself, casts his eye over the largely positive reviews that are gathered in a folder. 'Razor-sharp portrayal of society's dark side', 'brutal beauty'. That kind of thing. His rage builds. He's drunk, tired. He smashes the glass table. His son comes in, rubbing sleep from his eyes. Defends himself. Insults his father. He says: 'Who are you to criticise me, who are you to lay claim to this story? It's my life too, those letters intruded on my life. Your actions, your fucking verdict, your fucking sentence, they're a part of my life, of what has shaped my life. Who are you? Who are you to come here and demand loyalty? You should be glad your pathetic life has become art and made something of value for once.' Then the father loses his head and beats his son to death. And vanishes, despairing. The next morning, the son's mother comes to visit. She finds her child dead, falls to her knees and lifts his head, cursing the man, as she has done so many times before.

Yeah, those scenes were the foundation, the central part. The rest was filler, flesh, it was there to give life, stability, to hold up the construction. But I don't know if it succeeded. It collapses as soon as I've built it up. I build it up again, and it collapses. And I build it up again and it collapses again. Every time. I build it up again, and again, and again, and again, and again, and again.

TWELVE TALES ON THE ART OF BUILDING BRIDGES

1. Zero: Wandering Stars

The visible part of a story always begins with a stem. The stem of this story is a journey. Just an ordinary journey. Travel. To travel, to be going somewhere, always implies that borders are crossed. Small and large, visible and invisible, insignificant and momentous.

Here, someone is taking the train across a border. The uniformed guard says *Thank you, madam*, when the person shows their papers, their passport: *Thank you, Miss Smith. Miss Kovač. Miss Hadad.*

This someone, called *Hesin, Gowas, Demirci* in this case, returns their documents to their plastic case, their handbag, their backpack, their suitcase, with a deceptively calm appearance, and looks out through the window of the train. She sees the hypnotic movements – everyone has seen them, she thinks – concrete, stone, and rails, posts, signs and lights swishing past. The heavy, slanting cables that cut into your field of vision, rhythmically, stretched in a way that indicates a purpose of some kind, a function.

And then the sea, all the tones of blue in the colourless water, the black-blue patches in the gentle ripples – the cloudy-day blankets of greyness and the surf's white foam. Everyone has experienced that draw, she thinks, the dissolution of finitude that goes back thousands of years. Everyone is familiar with it, or so she wants to believe. Everyone knows, or so she hopes.

Her journey can also be described as an odyssey, an epic saga, a road movie – something other than the everyday crossing of a border – perhaps something to tell your children and grandchildren about, the other future children of the future, when they want to understand their so-called roots. Or, if not understanding, at least seeing, if not seeing, at least feeling, sensing, hoping.

Of course, this understanding is no mean feat for those who are hungry for truth, who want to get beyond the illusory, the automated. The blindness of familiarity, the routine. And presumably, it doesn't get any easier for them when they find an old diary in an unremarkable-looking cardboard box and read:

'Who was it who said they had a pain in their roots? Is that trite, sentimental? I don't know if I even understand the root metaphor. I don't have the past under me, or even behind me, for that matter, but inside me, and it's concentrated in the upper part of my body, let's say the heart, or the lungs, and upwards. Between the eyes and the back of the head, in the central nervous system, in the amygdala – somewhere there I have what could be described by the word roots. And sure, sometimes it hurts, but mostly it doesn't, and sometimes it just feels heavy, which is to say – it's pulled downwards by gravity, or outwards, away from me, like it's influenced by the gravitational force of some other planet that's invisible to me.'

The roots make themselves felt. The stem forks in two.

The story
    divides into two parts
    which are not reunited before they too
    divide into two parts
    which are likewise not reunited
    until it all ends.

It is a basic prerequisite of hers, that
    she *is* what she is not, and that

she *is not* what she is.
It's this double-ness,
It's this border-life –
that is this tale's
two-fold core.

Someone calls themselves *Schmidt, Pereira, Kuznetsova* and sits on a train travelling between two cities. The train could also be described as a bridge, the cities as planets. The bridge could be described as a wall. The planets as wandering stars. Since we are viewing this from our own planet, there are three planets, three wandering stars. Then things progress quickly from graspable to incalculable. Most cosmological epochs cannot be conceived of, not by any mind.

Primordial, Stelliferous, Degenerate, Black Hole, Dark Era.

But she has to have something to hold on to. Time, movement, form, and then suddenly a calendar. Roman, Islamic, Julian. 4 February. 24 May. 9 November. 1582. 1753. 18 April 1940.

She is three years old. She is twelve, thirteen, fifteen years old. The adults call her *Kowalska, Herrero, Kuznets* and give her water that seeps between her fingers. She wants to drink but doesn't dare. And then it's gone.

Forgetting, the inescapable seeping, the tension between stillness and movement: 'What happened is happening, again and again.'

This is important: a construction that connects always has an aspect that separates, an aspect that fills the body with border-life. With death-life, with a death-world. With exceptions and invalidation – from simple verbal misunderstandings to animalistic languagelessness. From there it's a long way to spacious words like life and world, border-life and death-world. It's always someone else talking, then.

4 June 1964. No one here can understand how the atom relates to the word. Or the image. But she collects the words and the images, the rhythms and the melodies, and she sorts them, memorises them.

She stands there. In the park, in the harbour, in the shopping centre. And imagines how her ventricle is pumping, colourless in the darkness, intelligent, actively expelling.

Time is crystalline here, she knows that. Solid, hard.

There is a hatred that moves southwards, eastwards. She, in the other direction. 10 December 1981 at a border point. Everything has been shattered, there is nothing left to protect any more. She is an adult and has black discolouration under her skin, on her wrists, her hands. It is early morning but she has already spoken to her father and answered his unspoken question:

I don't remember any day long ago.

I will never make use of your memories.

Her bronchial tree blossoms and bears fruit: red, dripping berries over the whiteness of teeth that are far from white. Her mother's arms like trunks, in her memory, fingers like branches, the leaves are already on the ground beneath her, along with the berries' seeds, still glistening with juice.

I will never be able to deal with the disappearance, she thinks. Or the legacy, to inherit an impossibility and then carry it with you through life, pulled tight, from your forehead, over your scalp and neck, over your shoulders and back, the fears a plume that stretches up and out. Regardless of where the compass is positioned.

The stems, the branches, the twigs. The trees, the streets, the cities. She remembers a friend and the contours of his Adam's apple, his long, thin neck, the dark brown hair that curled at the ends. It's an evening in July or August at the beginning of the nineties. They're standing outside the central station, he's on his way to Copenhagen, deep into a benzo-high (you're smiling at me behind veils of Stesolid, she thinks). He looks happy and messed up. The Danes, he says, they know how to live. I hate Sweden.

The surface and underside of the road bridge, double-exposed onto future starry skies. She sees spectres drift forth between the houses. You and I, she thinks, the pain that united us unites us no longer, but our bodies will never forget – however unreal that may seem.

The streets, the farms, the lawns, the way we glide through the summer evening, so close to both tenderness and a thing that is definitively violent. But I'm happy now, and you at least seem to be.

It's just a memory. Here and now the sun is setting and night has come. The sun rises and her eyes can't keep her vision straight. All impressions escape her. It's what comes from inside that embeds itself.

She knows she has enemies and she knows that her enemies have their planets, their centres of gravity. And she has had her own, but no longer, now it's as though she was born outside that crystalline place – time's out of step, as though she was the result of a three-month-long labour, a decades-long delivery, centuries of movement, eternity behind, inside, and in front of her.

An enormous, flat surface full of very small holes.

Someone is given a name, it's always a new name. Again and again, a little like everyday life. Milk flowing over the children's teeth and chopping in the kitchen. That thing about staple foods, basic commodities, spices and fruits (she describes the fruits of her childhood: gooseberries – picked too early, sour, with a white coating; currants – red, black, clusters of pearls; strawberries – we sit on our haunches in the strawberry patch and pick them one by one, blowing off any soil and popping them into our mouths, or into a bucket we give to Grandma, who rinses and picks them over, puts them in a bowl with sugar and smetana; cherries – small and dark red, I filled my mouth, crushing them, then stood in front of the mirror and let the blood-like juice run from the corners of my mouth). She sees her body as she looks out through the window. Her eyes have already cast themselves down, her hands do not move, her hands are threatening. I am old and forgotten, she feels, I lack a voice but can clearly see how the trees are listening for something. And now we're passing the bridge.

I can't see anyone out there, in the open.

It's dawn and they lead her into a little interrogation room, she remembers someone saying that it's there the soul becomes most visible, that it checks itself somehow, and becomes opaque. It would be due to the fear. The amygdala again. Experiences that open themselves. Blossom-shaped traces on the skin. Plumes, foliage, moss. Trees, trees, trees, and on. Both falling asleep and waking up should follow clear paths, even if these don't exist. The questions should be felt on your skin, every question either a skeleton key or a real one. Everyone meets in untruth in the end. In the good lie, the motivating one, the whitening, weightless lie. The true one.

This life has taught her to count. It protects her from the uniforms and from the tunnel vision of her heart. She pretends she is the furious rain, that she is the posts. She carries her legacy, and it feels like standing on the palms of one's own hands and lifting oneself up. She has a body and it is sleeping under a warmth as grey as fields. Tries to convince herself that everyone has travelled across a bridge, everyone has seen a wall, been invisible, touched. Everyone will die. The compulsion is singular and eternal. It is important. All this will die.

She will move in the world again, among its fruits.

It's no fucking game, this. And still it's like playing sometimes, you have to win, to make headway, gather, find ways, get through room after room, track after track, boss after boss.

And at that point it's impossible to avoid being turned into entertainment. Everything is a game, an act. Some have to suffer so that others can play, build an aesthetic around the problems of suffering, a career. Some get names, others give them.

Now we're here, the forks have reached their limit, she has finally forgotten the names, all of them, and so much else. When the fantasies have nowhere else to go, they take on the coarse surface of the white wall. She gets drunk on the things, on counting them. The unusually dim light from the TV lights up three figures on their knees, hands clasped and praying for peace. Again. The warmth inside, inside life. The gestures seep forth, through the day. Uncontrolled thoughts. Existence streams out across floors and furnishings.

Why is it so hard to understand what's holy here?

Cores, branches, stems. A sun. Fruits, stones, seeds.

We are still travelling, on the wandering star.

Before her a storm, flowering season.

'We are already on the other side.'

2. Stonemason

My dad was a stonemason. I mean, he didn't do that much stonema-sonry here, he was mostly a cleaner. But he'd trained as a stonemason. Back home. When we were little he used to tell me and my siblings things about the craft. He'd give long sermons about bricks and stone. How long, wide and deep they had to be, depending on what they were being used for. And he could describe in detail different techniques for making, like, corners and windows or various kinds of ornamentation. He loved to talk about arches in particular. I remem-ber it as almost a kind of song, his way of saying things like *segmental arch* and *transverse arch, springer, voussoir* and *keystone*, or phrases like *the lancet arch, in which the crown and the springer form a perfect, equilateral triangle,* or *the wonderful relationship between the radius, the span and the spring point in a horseshoe arch.*

Maybe one day you'll understand, he might say to us kids, the enor-mous efforts, both intellectual and physical, that have been required, throughout the ages, just for you to be able to go through a door, open a window, or stand on a floor. You know, he said, it's this that is the wonder of the quotidian. Yes, that's really how he spoke to us.

And then he would start on the mortar. Which ingredients you needed — he had a few secret ones too, which he would reveal when the time was right — and how you mixed everything to get the right consistency. But the most important thing of all was how you wielded the trowel. Your movements had to be *nonchalant but precise.*

You see, he'd say, levity and complexity are two sides of the same thing. Like order and chaos. The good life. And you have to look on the bright side, regardless of how dark it is. A few lines from a simple yet wise stonemason.

And we listened and reluctantly imagined how it would feel to put one stone on top of another for days on end. Perhaps it was our fate to complete what he started.

Is this what our name means, I asked once.

He shrugged then, and said:

No, my child. It means 'smith'.

3. *Words*

I spent my first, anxious time in this country in a white room with a large window and herbs growing on the windowsill. There was a mattress, a desk, a chair and a very old, slow laptop. Mostly, if I wasn't sitting on the chair, at the desk, attempting to write on the laptop, I lay on the mattress and read books and waited. One book – it was written by a Latin American *or* a Belgian author I can no longer remember the name of – was about some kind of house, and two types of people who lived in this house, or in this village, or town, or region. It was about how similar they were, despite being totally different. At least I think it was, I can't exactly remember the story. Nor the title. In actual fact I remember so little I probably shouldn't have brought it up at all. But there was one detail I remember very clearly. You see, at some point while reading this book I came across a word I'd never seen before. The word was 'parallellepiped'. I had no idea what a parallellepiped was, and it wasn't really clear from the text either. There was no dictionary in my room and I had no internet connection. I remember reading that passage with the parallellepiped again and again, and I said the word parallellepiped aloud to myself, repeating it as though its meaning would somehow come to me. I gave it colours and characteristics, decorated it: skilled parallellepiped, blue parallellepiped, drug-induced parallellepiped, green parallellepiped, white, azure, violet parallellepiped, round, sparkling, warm parallellepiped. I opened a new document on the laptop, which took eighteen minutes to start up, and made a list of all conceivable meanings. A dance? A bridge? An occupation? A psychological phenomenon that in some way encompasses telepathy, visions and children? I didn't know. One day I summoned all my courage and asked a neighbour, who I'd previously spoken to on the stairs, if he knew what the word meant. At first he made a face as if to suggest I was messing with him, but when he realised I was serious, that it was important to me, he said he'd try to assist me with my problem. The next day there was a knock on my door. I got up from the mattress and opened it. My neighbour was standing there with his wife. They looked really happy. I felt my own face light up too, for some reason. The woman handed me a piece of green rubber – about half the size of my thumb.

Parallellepiped, she said.

I looked at the piece of rubber.

OK, said the man. Have a good day.

I felt disappointed and ridiculous.

Same to you, I managed to stammer. And thanks.

They nodded and went on their way. I sat on my chair and put the parallellepiped on the desk next to the laptop. I looked at it and felt how my anxiety, very slowly, began to drain away.

4. Night Light

There are many of us who like to lie awake late into the night and feel how everyone else is sleeping, how everything is still, resting and waiting. Whether it's the night that is waiting for the day to come with its light and its movements, its exaggerated focus on activity, its throngs, its cacophony; or if the reverse is true – that it's the day, now inactive and at rest, that is waiting for the night to withdraw, to move on to other places, where others are lying awake – we have no way of knowing. But we know we're not allowed to stay in this feeling for too long, since there's a risk that the scales will fall from our inner eyes, and we will begin to suffer. To suffer so much we're forced to get up and do all we can to find something other than the life awaiting us with the dawn.

That is what we sometimes call the dark night of the soul.

5. Birds

There are two children on a balcony, looking at birds. The swallows fly low, the gulls copulate, rubbing cloaca against cloaca. The swallows appear to be hunting something or fleeing something. One gull stands on top of the other and both of them shriek. The children's knowledge of animal behaviour is limited, perhaps because they are children. They are siblings and they are skiving school, which has been burned down anyway. The sister has a dart she stole, or simply borrowed, from a neighbour. The dart has a sharp point at one end, and four wings, which are also flags, at the other. The brother thinks it's the USA's flag, but the sister thinks it's England's.

'I want to throw it at a bird,' she says.

'At a white or a black one?' he asks.

'All the same to me,' she says. 'It's not the feathers that matter when you throw a dart at a bird.'

6. Event

To begin with everything was fine, but after a while an event occurred that we subsequently referred to as The Event. We dealt with The Event to the best of our abilities and soon everything was fine again, except in a different way. Some people even started saying that everything hadn't really been fine at all before The Event, and that we were actually better off now, and so we should be grateful to The Event and celebrate it instead of moaning and slapping our palms on our foreheads and singing laments as many of us did on the anniversary of The Event. But then many people said that The Event wasn't even an event, that nothing had happened, everything was fine, aside from the fact that some of us insisted on either celebrating or bemoaning an event that was completely imaginary.

7. Other Sides

A hat in Beirut. Clouds, shadows and rivers. A camp site in Antwerp. Dumb masculinity, threats. Exodus, the flight from Egypt, hijra. The bridge, the wall and the abyss. The cello in Novgorod. The girl who sang Psalm 13 accompanied by a slightly out-of-tune steel-string guitar – *How long will you hide your face from me?* The cembalo at the student's place in Mannheim. Poplars, linden and oaks. Chestnuts, elms and maples. Bridges, walls and fences. Bridges, walls and land. Fairuz, Věra Bílá. Cities, parks and streets. Grandpa Dušan, who looked out across the motorway bridges and the hot cardboard roofs of the low houses (was it really cardboard? Have I only dreamed it?) and formulated his vision: *One day all this will come tumbling down.* An unfamiliar song on a stage. Elm, bird cherry and hazelnut. Maple, pussy willow and linden. A dying species, melting ice. Cats, dogs and birds. One day the bridges will fall. Proper old alcoholic; so I'll be a bird. Look for a perch. Evening prayers at dusk and dirty hands, they roll a ball of hash between distracted fingers. The concrete, the night and the colours. Gates, doors and stairs. Doors, rugs and sofas. We sit and lie on the floor. Chairs, wooden tables and plastic trays. Glasses, bottles and hands. Nights, stars and the universe. The children in bed in the next room and a voice whispering: Sleep now, little bear. Rest, you'll need your strength tomorrow. Everything can exist. And more than everything does exist. One day the walls will come tumbling down, they said. We stood there once, on the other side. We'll stand there one day, on the other side. A family is separated by the war. A life full of love that violence suffocated. Humans are the only beings who can take something so simple and make it impossible. One day they'll ask us for help to get to the other side, and we'll tell them: Friends! You're already on the other side.

8. Place

There. You see there. You see. Right there. Right. Between the rocks and the bridge supports. In the gap in between. Just exactly right there. Exactly there. In between. I can't comprehend it. I can't. It's impossible to comprehend. Impossible. Just there. Exactly there. There, by the rocks and there by that support. Right. You see. Exactly. That's where we used to swim when I was little. Or when I was a teenager. That's where we swam. We were little. And now. I can't get my head around it. Now it's, well, what is it? It's impossible to comprehend. Now everything is different. It's unimaginable. And yet the same. I really can't get my head around it. Then. And now. Right here. When I was a child. When I was growing up. You see there. That we swam there. You see. Exactly. We swam. There, between the supports and the rocks. Although they weren't there then. Not the supports. Not even the rocks. There was nothing there. Only water. And us. Swimming. Right here, it was. The bridge didn't exist. Only we existed. Just here. And the water. But not the same water. Not even that. Different water. It's impossible to get your head around it. I can't comprehend it. Right here. Exactly here. Exactly right here. In the gap in between. Between the rocks and the bridge supports. That weren't here. Exactly. Right here. You can see it now. You see here. Here.

9. Headwords

On 4 August 2016, in a gallery in Berlin, not far from Brandenburger Tor, where that old union leader Reagan gave his famous *Tear Down This Wall* speech, Schmidt is introduced to two wealthy Australians, Mr and Mrs Wallace ('Are you Swedish, I never would have guessed'). When she tells them she lives in Malmö, they respond enthusiastically that they know Malmö. That's where you go shopping when you're in Copenhagen. They say they visited Copenhagen a few months previously in their yacht. Schmidt, who's suffering from severe toothache at the time, is indisposed to small talk, so she nods politely and says something obliging about exchange rates and then goes to stand in front of one of the texts on the gallery wall. She experiences a mild sense of vertigo as she tries to read the text, a kind of doubled zooming-in-and-out that makes her think of the dolly zoom scene in Mathieu Kassovitz's film *La Haine*. Schmidt leaves the gallery, gets her bike, and wanders around aimlessly, looking at things in shop windows. She closes her eyes and hears the clattering of a café and a juicer, banging and crashing, fragments of music; she hears a muted beat, pop and high soul singers, children's voices. Then she cycles home, takes two painkillers. In the evening, she gets out her computer and looks up the word *imagination*.

Imagination is the ability to mentally conjure things you haven't experienced {→ day-dreaming, delusions, escapism}: imaginary friends; imaginary visions; imaginary worlds; unimaginative; capturing the imagination; creative imagination; give your imagination free rein and improvise. Dream imagery.

10. Siblings

Excerpts from the tale of the orphaned conjoined twins Aje and Eja:

All people carry with them nightmares and phantoms. If these cannot be contained in one's own body, one must send them out into the world so they can take up residence in other people. It's a common assumption that what is normal is pure and perfect. Children without parents are not normal. And two siblings who are attached are neither pure nor normal nor perfect.

[---]

During their upbringing in the children's home, Aje and Eja related to the other children in the same way the children's home related to the world outside. As a deplorable exception. In the world outside the children's home there were children who had parents. In the children's home there were children who were not attached to their siblings. Aje and Eja were attached and had no parents. Someone must always be impure and imperfect and abnormal. There are rumours to be spread and they have to be about someone. There are stones to be thrown and there has to be somebody for them to hit.

[---]

There are things that can be neither seen, heard nor held. There are things that keep people together, lead them from themselves to themselves, over invisible bridges, through secret doors and hidden cracks.

11. Legacy

In other people's eyes she was nothing more than an insignificant old woman. An elderly individual who needed help opening doors and carrying bags, who was incapable of climbing stairs and moved much too slowly along corridors and narrow pavements. They probably didn't even see her face, with its vacant, slightly sunken eyes and skin that could barely conceal the pale blue-green twigs and branches of her circulation.

What they saw — the contours of a frail person unable to take care of herself or offer much of value anywhere — sometimes made them think of those old German drawings of the steps of life, *from the cradle to the grave*, where the journey from infantile to senile was just eight steps long. The steps were not uncommonly represented as a bridge over the river of life, or as the tree of life, in which divine creatures sometimes lay resting in the cool shadows.

They never got to see her like I saw her. Reclining calmly in her old armchair with a cup of tea close at hand, or a Coca-Cola with ice and a slice of lemon. Her hands folded on her lap.

That's how she would tell her stories. She who had always taken care of everyone and everything. The oldest of five siblings. Times of war and famine. She who had survived occupation, dictatorship and a tyrannical spouse. Was she bitter, aggrieved, sorrowful, tired? Yes, sometimes. Was she mean, narrow-minded and xenophobic? Yes, sometimes. And at other times, full of strength. Grateful, tender and generous.

She told her stories with a force, an obstinacy, that she otherwise lacked. And she always ended them by giving me a satisfied look and saying,

Well? What will you give me for that one?

12. *Apeiron (Zero)*

Every day I think the war has not yet started. Here. The war hasn't yet reached here.

Over everything: a sky, low clouds, lit by a hidden sun. In the distance, above the horizon, a dark, dense forest. Yesterday, late morning, I sat here at my desk and watched as a great flame fell down towards the treetops. It left a gently curving tail of smoke behind it and went out just above the trees. A star? A starting pistol? Then came another, this one climbed higher, blazed brighter, but went out more quickly. And another. And one more. I counted six in total. They must be many kilometres away. Was someone trying to communicate something? I sat immobile at my desk. Who here is unreachable?

Water runs beneath the forest: black, blue, colourless, grey. Reflected light, shadows. Parts of the water are hidden by the tops of the pines, flame-coloured roof tiles with black and green patches and an ochre façade. Echoes of that yellow can be seen in the pale branches of the pines; crooked, downwards-bending branches. The trunks grey, partly covered with ivy. On the ground at their base, a tear in the landscape and a hole, an abyss as though left by a monstrous blow.

Today everything is laughable, if even that. How to process it, how to be? What to do?

Apeiron, it says on a piece of paper in the library reading room — that boundlessly unbounded space.

Boundlessness: that without outer boundaries — the spatially infinite — and that without internal boundaries.

All things originate in the boundless.

We're on our way there.

ONE LAST
ANECDOTE

Dad! It was such a sick feeling when I went to see my little bro and we stood on the walkway outside his flat and

I don't know if you been there, if you been where he lives, but

we were standing there looking out over the yard and the streets, the sky was dark and the light was like warm and cold at the same time, like it gets sometimes, and he tells me about how he conned a shop into giving him this little blow-up pool by swapping the price tags and going to the tills and acting all threatening when the staff questioned this mad low price, and you know how it is, he's the world's sweetest, gentlest guy, but the minute you got a bit of an accent, just a tiny little bit: caca in their pants, right away.

I know, you don't know about this stuff, you always have an accent, I know, and we laugh at you, and Mum, behind your backs, after we been helping you, interpreting for you or translating the forms, the instructions and information sheets for you, and no, we're not laughing *with* you, we're really laughing *at* you if I'm gonna be totally honest, Dad, since we can speak proper German if we want, or when we need to, and it's beautiful German, proper Standarddeutsch, proper fucking Hochdeutsch, ja? and it's so fucking easy to switch, change, jump from one to the other, you just like, move the weight in your tongue, or what am I saying, of your tongue – anyway, you do a thing with your tongue, nothing fancy, drop a letter, emphasise a vowel, swallow another, move a word here and a word there, and suddenly your sentences have a different meaning and a totally different effect. It's like magic, yeah? And we've always been little magicians, all of us, so it was no biggie for my brother to magic down the price of that fucking pool. Then he and Dani carried it up to the roof of their nine-storey building and inflated it with a machine they borrowed off some mate. And they hooked up a hose from their bathroom and filled the pool with water, which took its sweet time, like a few hours, I swear. And my brother told me how everyone in the building loved that pool, they hung out up there all summer long, they had like pool parties with views right across Alter Elbpark and half of the Reeperbahn, they had DJs and rappers who played for free, like Ahzumjot, OG Keemo, and Trettmann or whoever, and word got out about that fucking pool and this roof, and people came from like Berlin and Hanover and Munich and Cologne to get in on it. This one time, a big bunch of Poles even came over from Poznań, so Peja from Slums Attack could record a video or a scene in some film.

All because of this little blue plastic pool that was big enough for like four people. It was nuts, my brother said. You know, people came who had access to proper roof terraces and actual fucking jacuzzis and shit, people with money, serious shotters and heavies, so in the end it was almost too much, you get me, like, too much of a good thing, you know, the cops started showing up and there were rumours of plain clothes, and people started getting nervous, and it was the kind of people you want to avoid when they get nervous, if you know what I mean. It wasn't like people got in the pool, most of them just stood round, hung out, like you do in summer, chatting shit, smoking green, drinking beer or cocktails, eating hot dogs or barbecue, you know. There were a few Latinos who lived in the building who knocked up a proper asado a few times. Have you ever been to a real asado? So much meat you can't believe it. Beef heart on skewers, delicious. But luckily autumn came, and by mid-September no one wanted to stand around freezing their arses off any more, so the whole thing ran its course. But we hung around a few weekends more, Dani and me, and a few others, sitting reminiscing and telling stories and looking at that pale blue plastic pool which had got totally gross and filthy because we couldn't be fucked to clean it towards the end, and we just thought, fuck, what a total ride, what a mindfuck that this could even happen.

The best summer since we were teenagers, he said, and I believed him, easily. I could see it in front of me, even though it was night now, it was properly dark and summer was definitely over.

That feeling, Dad! Standing there in the dark, lighting a cigarette and feeling a tiny bit wasted. Feeling that brotherhood and joking about going back to yours and landing you one, beating you up, killing you, and forcing my tiny, tiny sons, my twins, to come along, getting them to give you a few hard slaps right at the end.

That feeling. As we were standing on the walkway, laughing and shaking our heads at all the bastards we'd come into contact with, seeing the blue lights blaze past down there, and my brother told me how he and Dani were about to steal a bike one time and some nutjob cop turned up from nowhere with his gun drawn, and everyone panicked, but Dani just put his hands up and said to the cop:

You reckon you're in Compton, or something?

and everyone started laughing their arses off, and more and more cops came and they all realised the first cop had gone way too far, so they let them go.

They let us steal that bike, you get me, just so we wouldn't report the stuff about the gun. Back then it wasn't cool to pull a gun on unarmed teenagers apparently.

And then we stayed out there on the walkway, talking about the word *walkway* and then I wheeled out that story I always wheel out about us running around with a loaded pistol in Harburg – it was me, Saša, Novák and Vincent, and maybe someone else, maybe Shimmy, I don't remember exactly – because we were scared of the skinheads there. We'd gone there cos Novák was off to meet some girl, plus Saša wanted to sell grass. And the party was totally wild, but everyone really was shit-scared of these fucking Nazis. I guess it was partly because the people there were like communists and autonomists, and then I guess there were a few, not many, but a few, ghetto kids

and Saša got pissed off and started going off on one at some of them – some bitch was standing on the roof, waving this massive Soviet flag, and his grandma was one of the people killed in the Berlin uprising in 1953, they shot her in the head, the cops, she was a Slovakian Roma who fled to East Germany at the beginning of the fifties, I've only heard a bit about her life, but it's a fucking bizarre story, I reckon, that someone should tell properly some time, the story of Jozefína S, the revolutionary partisan from the Tatra Mountains

plus that was his thing, selling grass to students and trying to destroy their arguments, but in the end we all crashed out in a school playground and woke up when it started raining the next morning.

I don't know, actually

I don't know why I wheeled out that story, I don't know why I always wheel it out, there's nothing special about it, I guess it's just because that bit about the gun, the pistol, it makes it feel dangerous, or exciting, I don't know, to be honest it mostly stresses me out to think we were once a bunch of idiotic little kids running around with a loaded gun. 'Let me hold it. Let me. Give it, give it here. My go, give it here, man.'

Make sure the safety's on, keep your finger on the side of the barrel and not on the trigger, point the muzzle at someone's head. Nothing can happen. And yet, that feeling.

I don't know.

But it felt good to stand there and chat shit with my brother, and of course I told him about the pub crawls with you, Dad, since he hadn't heard all of it yet, apparently. That part surprised me actually, everyone loves talking so fucking much. At least that's what I thought. But apparently there are still things left to go over, to grind on about, to wheel out, again and again, it never ends, damn it, as I've already said thousands of times, and a thousand times again. Not to you, maybe, but to friends, girlfriends, brothers and sisters. School counsellors and psychologists. Again and again you wheel out these stories and see them transformed, twisted, changing shape. They get stronger or weaker, the colours fade or get more intense, the perspectives shift, recalibrate.

The brain is a weird thing, Dad. It's impossible to get your head around, if you get what I mean. It's impossible to get your head around this need to share, to spread the word or whatever. I don't know, Dad. I don't know why I wheeled out that one about the time we smoked a fat one in that little bar on the corner, you know, when that girl I was with then, who worked there, Heike, was so impressed, in that twisted fucking way middle-class kids always are, because she's never seen a parent smoking with their child before, and then you blacked out at the bar and I had to carry you home. Up that narrow old wooden staircase. You remember it? That creaky old wooden staircase. Course you do. And the unheated kitchen, and the stove in the big room, which we fed with stinking coal briquettes. I actually thought it smelled good too, in a way: homey, cosy, even though that smell came with the insults, the degradation, the humiliation. The self-loathing that was so huge there wasn't space for it in your body. You were compelled to rub it off on us, a sick and unhappy compulsion that, admittedly, would flip to the reverse the following day, to regret and anxious tenderness. Our version of cosiness. As the old song goes: *Home is where the hatred is*, right Dad?

And do you remember that fat old woman who hung out in her window all day long with her cushion and her nightdress? She called it a *négligée* once, when someone, I think it was my sister, dissed her, and her old man started roaring something from his spot in front of the TV with his beer and his greasy wurst. Négligée. It sounded so awesome with a German accent and her throat-cancer voice. That staircase, Dad. That house. Have I ever told you that I broke in there one night after they'd emptied it, a few months after they made you move, back in the early nineties when everything started changing and the money was rolling in, demanding its *Lebensraum*. Hotels and espresso machines and nice shops rolled in and the people left.

It was one night a few weeks before they tore the whole thing down. I climbed in through a broken window in the basement, went up the stairs and kicked open the door that still had our name on it, and then I stood there in the empty fourth-floor apartment where I'd been through it all, all those things. I just stood there in the darkness, it was so empty, there was nothing anywhere, just patches of light and shadow on the walls and ceiling, I stood there a long time, wandered around, it was totally unreal and I remember wanting to be in that unreality, that I wanted to stay and live in it instead of living in the real world. But I didn't know how, how do you do that? How do you do something like that, Dad? Stay in unreality. Like, I was already drunk and stoned, but that's never helped, you know? I thought I should fall asleep in the little toilet and lie there, curled up around the toilet itself, when they pulled the house down. No, nothing like that, I thought then. I should set fire to the whole house. Just burn it down. But I did nothing. Listened to music on my headphones, I think, and maybe smoked a straight. And then went home to the new apartment 200 metres away and said nothing to you.

But I wheeled all this out for my brother just now, while we stood on the walkway, feeling good, somehow, because of course he remembered the old apartment even if he was much smaller then, so young he didn't really get what it was all about, and he wheeled out a few stories of his own about you getting drunk in there, about how you put him down, really a lot of sick things I can't be bothered to go through now, you know what you did, even if you can't remember the events themselves, eh, Dad? And I wheeled out that one about the time you started on some heavy in the bar, at Heike's place, and I had to intervene and clean up the whole mess, save you. And then

I guess I wheeled out that whole long story about our trip back home, if you recall, which started

so calmly, and, how should I put it

intellectually, with politics, and history lessons, and a tranquil account of living conditions, I convinced myself it was about post-Marxism and historical materialism

but still it ended with you crashing out between some bins somewhere down by the river, and I climbed up on them and took some photos of you, and later, if you recall, when I got them developed, you tore up the pictures, without a word, but I know you were embarrassed that the whole thing got out of control — but I still have the negatives, it was back when people had real cameras, with film and that, you know, Dad, you know how it was, right?

And all this made me think about Matias and Mirko, who also went back to their home countries and their fathers. One, in Argentina, didn't give a fuck about Matias, he just opened the door, stood in silence for a few minutes while Matias tried to say something, and then went into the apartment, rummaged around in a drawer for a while before coming back with a thick envelope which he gave to Matias and said:

Here you are. Go away. Forget me. Don't come back.

No vuelvas

and shut the door and Matias opened the envelope and inside was several thousand dollars, a fat wad, he didn't count them, just stood there a long time, while those words, *No vuelvas*, echoed in his head like after a heavy blow, and he thought: what am I going to do, should I take the dough, cash is cash, right, or should I give it back, this is proper dirty money, this. Or should I burn it, or what?

You get it, his dilemma, right, Dad?

And Matias thought, he later told me, I'm going to take the fucking money and then I'm going to take a fucking taxi down to La Boca or Barracas, the tough parts of town, and then I'll fucking find someone to fix him up. Do him in.

He's going to fucking pay for his own death.

You know, he said this to me, and now he was smiling, because several years had already passed since this happened, I'd just seen a film about a guy who wants to die – he's going to kill himself, but he doesn't dare, you know, and he tries and fails several times, and in the end he goes to some low-level gangster and orders a hit, on himself, suicide by hit man, if you will, but something happens and I can't remember what, but anyway, he changes his mind, and this murderer hunts him down and so on, I can't fucking remember what the film is called either

he talks like this, Mati, always fucking up his stories with

I don't know, I can't remember

but anyway, he said to me, I took the cash, I took it, I stuffed the envelope down my pants and took the bus to the hotel and just sat there drinking Fernet and cola and smoking, thinking, or trying not to think, and waiting for Mariella, waiting for her to come home, or whatever you say when you're staying at a hotel, or, well, I say hotel, it was more like a hostel with no windows and this vile sewage stench in the toilet, and I don't know, but then she came in anyway, and she asked me how it went and at first I didn't say anything, or I said I don't know how it went, but then she said

what do you mean, don't know what

and then I said it didn't go that well, and then I told her everything apart from that bit about the money, like the actual

No vuelvas and all that

and the bus journey home, and the stress and how awful it felt, you know, and the whole time the envelope's sitting there, with the whole bundle, clearly visible on the bedside table beside her, and I looked at it several times, wondering if I should say something, almost hoping she would see it herself and pick it up and take out the bundle and look at me and ask me where the fuck this money came from, you get me, but she didn't see it, and in the end I couldn't be bothered any more and you know, I lost it

you know, right, you know how it is

but then we took the money home with us, I was pranging out going through customs, I don't know why, it felt like I'd stolen the shit, you know there was almost forty Gs there, dollars, we put them down as a deposit on our house later, and I think about how fucking freaked out the guy must have been when I just turned up one day like that, like a fucking ghost, shit he must have been scared, I mean, he was pretty flush, but still, putting so much cash into that, into my silence, and I could just as well have taken the money and still hounded him, still contacted his wife, his kids, my fucking siblings, right, my fucking family, and you know, I was planning to do that,

I thought as soon as I get home I'm going to send an email, go crazy on FB, write a letter, make a goddamn film and put it up on YouTube, you know, the whole business, but then I got home and I couldn't hack it, you know, I almost felt sorry for him, you get me, just imagine it, what a small person, what a vile little person, what a disgusting little disgusting bastard.

It's just disgusting, said Matías.

But you move on. You take a shower and you move on, he said.

Then the other dad, I told my brother, the one in Bulgaria, Mirko's dad.

Haralambi I remember his name was

Haralambi, he just cried, Mirko said

but on the sly, in secret.

He would turn around and leave the kitchen, cough, blow his nose, go to the toilet, but in the end he couldn't hide it, and he just cried, said Mirko, for like an hour, his false teeth tumbled out, his whole face collapsed, he just said my name, and *my boy, my boy*, trembling like an animal

Mirko Mirko, my boy, Mirko, Mirko Mirko, my boy, Mirko, my boy

repeating my name like a mantra, like a talking dog

took out a framed photo of me when I was like one, and showed me how he'd sat with it in the kitchen for thirty years, without a word

just my name, and *my boy, my boy*

it was so mental, Mirko said, in the end I thought he was going to die, I was just saying, there, there, there

I couldn't say Dad,

but I said there,

just there, there.

And it was a happy ending, I told my brother, because they hung out after that, he came to Mirko's wedding, and they went to football matches and grew peppers together and that, until he died of cancer a few years later.

I wheeled all this out as we were standing there in the walkway, and it really was a sick feeling, grinning and shaking our heads at everything, together

but in the end it got cold so we went inside and looked at some photos my brother had in an orange shoe box, and we listened to Kojey Radical and Rapsody and Kendrick's new one and I tried to explain to him why I think it's cool that Kendrick cried in public and on his recordings, but my brother didn't really get what I was saying so I just said it's cool, full stop, you're too young to get it, you think people are hard just because they act hard, but that's not it, the hardest thing is to *feel* the pain, to not be afraid of it, it's like Holyfield said, *if you can feel the pain, you still in the game.* I guess it sounded ridiculous, I guess it was ridiculous. But then my brother's room-mate came back – Petrovich, the Nicaraguan, and his buddy

I know, don't say it, it's a weird name for a Nicaraguan, and honestly I don't know how he spells it, but that's how it is with me and my people, everyone's weird in *some* way, especially in that national way

and they wanted us to come and smoke some stuff in their room, but we said no, it's cool, we're not up for that right now, but I chatted to them in Spanish, and asked them about their work at the docks, if it was hard graft and if it was poor pay and how their bastard bosses were, and then what kind of music they liked, if they read poetry, if there was a good poet from Nicaragua, and they shook their heads, and I said there must be at least one poet in Nicaragua worth reading, a Sandinista or something, and they said maybe, but we don't know, and then Petrovich said there's Ernesto Cardenal of course, but he's a priest, and apart from that they're all politicians, and I said I guessed priests were alright, but politicians were immediately excluded, and he agreed, yeah, that's a bullet in the back of the head right there, and then he said oh yeah there's that guy Óscar Romero too, but he was from El Salvador, and then we laughed and said yeah, he had nothing to do with it then, right, and his friend said that actually he didn't even write poetry, he was just a priest or a bishop, but then Petrovich got pissed off, and they started arguing, we heard how their discussion continued in his room, in front of his computer, where they probably googled the hell out of that shit, while my brother and I were taking it totally easy, just sipping the beer my sister had given us at the bar, several hours ago, and my brother showed me an IKEA shelf he'd sawn up so it would fit in a corner, and suddenly I started yawning and said I had to go now, cos my tiny little sons are going to wake up soon, and life goes on, it has to, and my brother said he'd walk with me for a while and we went out and it was night and the streets were full of pimps and johns and whores and motherfuckers and he told me more and more about how it was to grow up surrounded by prostitutes, an experience we hadn't shared, since I took off so early. It's like an avalanche, I thought, it grows and accelerates and carries on growing and becomes more and more and more the whole time. It's like a fever, it just gets hotter and hotter until it can't any more but then it still carries on

and my brother, my little brother, went on talking about how it had felt to see the other kids get sold and sell themselves, and in the middle of all this we often realise what fucking luck we've had, he said, because it could have been much worse, and there are loads of people who've been through things you can't even imagine, our sisters who we were never able to protect from the worst of it, and we walked along and I thought it *almost*, but only *almost*, feels like you don't want to live any more, and we walked and talked, because you *have* to live, as we always say

and I don't know, but I guess now I can stop pretending I'm saying all this to you, Dad, because you and I don't talk to each other, do we, we never have, or at least not in a really long time

I'm just sitting here, saying all this to myself, down into the bottle and the glass and the table top, that's the cold, hard truth, because I'm alone, because my tiny little sons, the twins, aren't so tiny any more, and they're not talking to me right now, for a whole heap of reasons, I'm guessing, but maybe mostly because of this very glass, this bottle, and the lines and tablets that unfortunately put in an appearance now and then, and because of all that other stuff, the stuff I can't talk about, the dark nights, and I miss my brother who died last year, and I miss having someone to talk to and I can't let go of the way we used to walk and walk and talk and talk

and I can't let go of that feeling and I can't stop thinking that it was a special feeling, a really sick feeling, being able to talk, not being afraid, and we walked and walked and in some ways we're still walking through the night, through those rain-soaked black streets that glisten and shine so nicely, and we're chatting and chatting, trying to get to something, something final perhaps, a final story maybe, something that can save us from reality, a final tale, one last, decisive anecdote, that would take away all the hardness, the rage, that could comfort us a little and make the contemplation and all this chatting and all this thinking, and all these exercises in the art of remembering and agonising, of being tortured by words and images and voices and voices and voices, and vague feelings in your gut and your chest, in your arms and legs and head, make all this superfluous, take away the words and the thoughts and the voices, lift us up beyond them, something that could open us up in some

way, like ripe fruits, maybe, cutting through our flesh and tearing out
the callouses, all the stuff that
    I don't know, I don't know
    all the stuff we don't know, maybe
    that thorn, maybe, the lump, the weight
    you know what I mean, maybe, whoever you are
    that pain, the scar
    the stuff that hurts the most
    in our slowly fading lives
    all the stuff the adults did
    when we were kids

Dear readers,

As well as relying on bookshop sales, And Other Stories relies on subscriptions from people like you for many of our books, whose stories other publishers often consider too risky to take on.

Our subscribers don't just make the books physically happen. They also help us approach booksellers, because we can demonstrate that our books already have readers and fans. And they give us the security to publish in line with our values, which are collaborative, imaginative and 'shamelessly literary'.

All of our subscribers:

- receive a first-edition copy of each of the books they subscribe to
- are thanked by name at the end of our subscriber-supported books
- receive little extras from us by way of thank you, for example: postcards created by our authors

BECOME A SUBSCRIBER,
OR GIVE A SUBSCRIPTION TO A FRIEND

Visit andotherstories.org/subscriptions to help make our books happen. You can subscribe to books we're in the process of making. To purchase books we have already published, we urge you to support your local or favourite bookshop and order directly from them – the often unsung heroes of publishing.

OTHER WAYS TO GET INVOLVED

If you'd like to know about upcoming events and reading groups (our foreign-language reading groups help us choose books to publish, for example) you can:

- join our mailing list at: andotherstories.org
- follow us on Twitter: @andothertweets
- join us on Facebook: facebook.com/AndOtherStoriesBooks
- admire our books on Instagram: @andotherpics
- follow our blog: andotherstories.org/ampersand

THIS BOOK WAS MADE POSSIBLE
THANKS TO THE SUPPORT OF

Aaron McEnery
Aaron Schneider
Abigail Walton
Ada Gokay
Adam Lenson
Adriel Levine
Ajay Sharma
Al Ullman
Alan Hunter
Alan McMonagle
Alasdair Cross
Albert Puente
Alcksi Rennes
Alex Fleming
Alex Ramsey
Alexander Bunin
Alexandra Stewart
Alexandria Levitt
Alfred Tobler
Ali Ersahin
Ali Riley
Ali Smith
Ali Usman
Alice Clarke
Alison Lock
Aliya Rashid
Allan & Mo Tennant
Alyssa Rinaldi
Alyssa Tauber
Amado Floresca
Amaia Gabantxo
Amanda
Amanda Milanetti
Amber Da
Amelia Dowe
Amine Hamadache
Amitav Hajra
Amos Hintermann
Amy and Jamie
Amy Hatch
Amy Lloyd
Amy Sousa
Amy Tabb

Ana Novak
Andrea Barlien
Andrea Larsen
Andrea Oyarzabal
   Koppes
Andreas Zbinden
Andrew Burns
Andrew Kerr-Jarrett
Andrew Marston
Andrew Martino
Andrew McCallum
Andrew Milam
Andrew Place
Andrew Place
Andrew Rego
Andrew Wright
Andy Marshall
Anna Finneran
Anna French
Anna Hawthorne
Anna Holmes
Anna Kornilova
Anna Milsom
Anna Zaranko
Anne Edyvean
Anne Frost
Anne Germanacos
Anne Ryden
Anne Willborn
Anne-Marie Renshaw
Annie McDermott
Anonymous
Ant Cotton
Anthony Cotton
Anthony Fortenberry
Anthony Quinn
Antonia Saske
Antony Pearce
April Hernandez
Archie Davies
Aron Trauring
Asako Serizawa
Ashleigh Sutton

Audrey Holmes
Audrey Small
Barbara Mellor
Barbara Spicer
Barry John Fletcher
Barry Norton
Becky Matthewson
Ben Buchwald
Ben Schofield
Ben Thornton
Ben Walter
Benjamin Judge
Benjamin Pester
Beth Heim de Bera
Beverley Thomas
Bianca Winter
Bill Fletcher
Billy-Ray Belcourt
Birgitta Karlén
Björn Dade
Bjørnar Djupevik Hagen
Blazej Jedras
Brandon Clar
Brendan Dunne
Briallen Hopper
Brian Anderson
Brian Byrne
Brian Callaghan
Brian Isabelle
Brian Smith
Bridget Prentice
Brittany Redgate
Brooke Williams
Brooks Williams
Buck Johnston & Camp
   Bosworth
Burkhard Fehsenfeld
Buzz Poole
Caitlin Farr Hurst
Caitlin Halpern
Callie Steven
Cameron Adams
Camilla Imperiali

Carl Emery
Carla Castanos
Carole Burns
Carole Parkhouse
Carolina Pineiro
Caroline Kim
Caroline Lodge
Caroline Montanari
Caroline Musgrove
Caroline Perry
Caroline West
Carolyn A Schroeder
Catharine Braithwaite
Catherine Jacobs
Catherine Lambert
Catherine McBeth
Catherine Tandy
Catherine Williamson
Cathryn Siegal-Bergman
Cecilia Rossi
Cecilia Uribe
Ceri Lumley-Sim
Cerileigh Guichelaar
Chandler Sanchez
Charles Fernyhough
Charles Heiner
Charles Kovach
Charles Dee Mitchell
Charles Rowe
Charlie Mitchell
Charlie Small
Charlotte Holtam
Charlotte Ryland
Charlotte Whittle
China Miéville
Chris Clamp
Chris Johnstone
Chris Lintott
Chris McCann
Chris Potts
Chris Senior
Chris Stergalas
Chris Stevenson
Christian Schuhmann
Christina Sarver
Christine Elliott
Christopher Fox

Christopher Stout
Ciara Callaghan
Claire Riley
Claire Williams
Clare Wilkins
Claudia Mazzoncini
Cliona Quigley
Colin Denyer
Colin Hewlett
Colin Matthews
Collin Brooke
Conor McMeel
Courtney Daniel
Courtney Lilly
Craig Kennedy
Cynthia De La Torre
Cyrus Massoudi
Daisy Savage
Dale Wisely
Daniel Cossai
Daniel Gillespie
Daniel Hahn
Daniel Jones
Daniel Sanford
Daniel Syrovy
Daniela Steierberg
Darcie Vigliano
Darren Boyling
Darren Gillen
Darryll Rogers
Darya Lisouskaya
Dave Lander
David Alderson
David Anderson
David Ball
David Eales
David Gray
David Greenlaw
David Gunnarsson
David Hebblethwaite
David Higgins
David Johnson-Davies
David Kaus
David F Long
David Miller
David Richardson
David Shriver

David Smith
David Smith
David Wacks
Dawn Walter
Dean Taucher
Deb Unferth
Debbie Pinfold
Deborah Green
Deborah McLean
Declan O'Driscoll
Delaina Haslam
Denis Larose
Denis Stillewagt & Anca
   Fronescu
Denise Brown
Derek Meins
Diane Hamilton
Diane Josefowicz
Dominic Bailey
Dominic Nolan
Dominick Santa
   Cattarina
Dominique Brocard
Dominique Hudson
Doris Duhennois
Dorothy Bottrell
Douglas Smoot
Dugald Mackie
Duncan Chambers
Duncan Clubb
Duncan Macgregor
Dustin Chase-Woods
Dyanne Prinsen
E Rodgers
Earl James
Ebba Tornérhielm
Ed Smith
Edward Champion
Ekaterina Beliakova
Eleanor Maier
Elif Aganoglu
Elina Zicmane
Elizabeth Atkinson
Elizabeth Balmain
Elizabeth Braswell
Elizabeth Cochrane
Elizabeth Draper

Elizabeth Franz
Elizabeth Leach
Elizabeth Rice
Elizabeth Seals
Elizabeth Sieminski
Ella Sabiduria
Ellen Agnew
Ellen Beardsworth
Ellie Goddard
Ellie Small
Emiliano Gomez
Emily Walker
Emma Bielecki
Emma Coulson
Emma Louise Grove
Emma Post
Emma Teale
Emma Wakefield
Eric Anderson
Erin Cameron Allen
Ethan White
Evelyn Reis
Ewan Tant
Fawzia Kane
Fay Barrett
Faye Williams
Felicity Le Quesne
Felix Valdivieso
Finbarr Farragher
Fiona Liddle
Fiona Quinn
Fiona Wilson
Fran Sanderson
Frances Dinger
Frances Harvey
Francesca Rhydderch
Frank Pearson
Frank Rodrigues
Frank van Orsouw
Gabriel Garcia
Gabriella Roncone
Gavin Aitchison
Gavin Collins
Gawain Espley
Gemma Alexander
Gemma Bird
Gemma Hopkins

Geoff Thrower
Geoffrey Urland
George McCaig
George Stanbury
George Wilkinson
Georgia Panteli
Georgia Shomidie
Georgina Hildick-Smith
Georgina Norton
Geraldine Brodie
Gerry Craddock
Gill Boag-Munroe
Gillian Grant
Gillian Spencer
Gina Filo
Glen Bornais
Glen Bornais
Glenn Russell
Gloria Gunn
Gordon Cameron
Gosia Pennar
Graham Blenkinsop
Graham R Foster
Grainne Otoole
Grant Ray-Howett
Hadil Balzan
Halina Schiffman-Shilo
Hannah Freeman
Hannah Harford-Wright
Hannah Jane
  Lownsbrough
Hannah Rapley
Hannah Vidmark
Hans Lazda
Harriet Stiles
Haydon Spenceley
Heidi Gilhooly
Helen Alexander
Helen Berry
Helen Mort
Henrietta Dunsmuir
Henrike Laehnemann
Holly Down
Howard Robinson
Hyoung-Won Park
Ian Betteridge
Ian McMillan

Ian Mond
Ian Randall
Ian Whiteley
Ida Grochowska
Ilya Markov
Inbar Haramati
Ines Alfano
Inga Gaile
Irene Mansfield
Irina Tzanova
Isabella Livorni
Isabella Weibrecht
Isobel Dixon
J Drew Hancock-Teed
Jack Brown
Jacob Musser
Jacqueline Haskell
Jacqueline Lademann
Jacqueline Vint
Jake Baldwinson
Jake Newby
James Avery
James Beck
James Crossley
James Cubbon
James Higgs
James Lehmann
James Leonard
James Portlock
James Richards
James Ruland
James Saunders
James Scudamore
James Silvestro
James Ward
Jamie Mollart
Jan Hicks
Jane Dolman
Jane Roberts
Jane Roberts
Jane Woollard
Janet Digby
Janis Carpenter
Jason Montano
Jason Timermanis
JE Crispin
Jeff Collins

Jeff Fesperman
Jeffrey Davies
Jen Calleja
Jen Hardwicke
Jennifer Fain
Jennifer Fosket
Jennifer Frost
Jennifer Harvey
Jennifer Mills
Jennifer Watts
Jennifer Yanoschak
Jenny Huth
Jeremy Koenig
Jeremy Sabol
Jerome Mersky
Jess Decamps
Jess Wood
Jessica Kibler
Jessica Queree
Jessica Weetch
Jethro Soutar
Jo Lateu
Joanna Luloff
Joanna Trachtenberg
Joao Pedro Bragatti
  Winckler
Jodie Adams
Joe Huggins
Joel Hulseman
Joel Swerdlow
Joelle Young
Johannes Menzel
Johannes Georg Zipp
John Berube
John Bogg
John Conway
John Gent
John Hodgson
John Kelly
John Miller
John Purser
John Reid
John Shaw
John Steigerwald
John Walsh
John Whiteside
John Winkelman

John Wyatt
Jolene Smith
Jon Riches
Jonathan Blaney
Jonathan Leaver
Jonathan Woollen
Joni Chan
Jonny Anderson
Jonny Kiehlmann
Jordana Carlin
José Echeverría Vega
Josephine Glöckner
Josh Glitz
Josh Sumner
Joshua Briggs
Joshua Davis
Joy Paul
Judith Gruet-Kaye
Julia Rochester
Julia Sutton-Mattocks
Julia Von Dem Knesebeck
Julie Atherton
Julie Greenwalt
Juliet Swann
Junius Hoffman
Jupiter Jones
Juraj Janik
Justine Sherwood
Kaarina Hollo
Kalina Rose
Kamaryn Norris
Karen Gilbert
Karen Mahinski
Katarzyna Bartoszynska
Kate Beswick
Kate Carlton-Reditt
Kate Rizzo
Katharine Robbins
Katherine Sotejeff-
  Wilson
Kathryn Edwards
Kathryn Williams
Kati Hallikainen
Katie Cooke
Katie Freeman
Katie Grant
Katrina Mayson

Katy Robinson
Keith Walker
Kelly Hydrick
Kelsey Grashoff
Kenneth Blythe
Kent McKernan
Kerry Broderick
Kerry Parke
Kieran Cutting
Kieran Rollin
Kieron James
Kirsten Benites
Kitty Golden
KL Ee
Kris Ann Trimis
Kristen Tcherneshoff
Kristen Tracey
Kristin Djuve
Kristy Richardson
Krystale Tremblay-Moll
Krystine Phelps
Kurt Navratil
Kyle Pienaar
Lana Selby
Laura Murphy
Laura Rangeley
Laura Zlatos
Lauren Pout
Lauren Schluneger
Lauren Trestler
Laurence Laluyaux
Leah Binns
Leda Brittenham
Lee Harbour
Leelynn Brady
Leona Iosifidou
Lex Orgera
Liliana Lobato
Lilie Weaver
Lily Blacksell
Linda Jones
Linda Whittle
Lindsay Attree
Lindsay Brammer
Lindsey Ford
Lisa Hess
Liz Clifford

Liz Ketch
Liz Ladd
Liz Wilding
Lorna Bleach
Louise Aitken
Louise Evans
Louise Jolliffe
Lucinda Smith
Lucy Moffatt
Luiz Cesar Peres
Luke Healey
Luke Murphy
Lydia Syson
Lyndia Thomas
Lynn Fung
Lynn Grant
Lynn Martin
Madalyn Marcus
Maeve Lambe
Maggie Livesey
Mandy Wight
Margaret Jull Costa
Mari-Liis Calloway
Maria Lomunno
Maria Losada
Marie Cloutier
Marijana Rimac
Marina Castledine
Marina Jones
Marion Pennicuik
Mark Grainger
Mark Reynolds
Mark Sargent
Mark Sheets
Mark Sztyber
Mark Tronco
Mark Troop
Mark Waters
Martha Wakenshaw
Martin Price
Mary Addonizio
Mary Clarke
Mary Heiss
Mary Tinebinal
Mary Wang
Mathias Ruthner
Matt Davies

Matthew Cooke
Matthew Crossan
Matthew Eatough
Matthew Francis
Matthew Lowe
Matthew Woodman
Matthias Rosenberg
Maxwell Mankoff
Maya Feile Tomes
Meaghan Delahunt
Meg Lovelock
Megan Wittling
Mel Pryor
Melynda Nuss
Michael Aguilar
Michael Bichko
Michael Boog
Michael Eades
Michael James Eastwood
Michael Floyd
Michael Gavin
Michael Parsons
Michael Schneiderman
Michele Whitfeld
Michelle Mercaldo
Michelle Mirabella
Miguel Head
Mike Abram
Mike James
Mike Schneider
Miles Smith-Morris
Mim Lucy
Miranda Gold
Mohamed Tonsy
Molly Foster
Molly Schneider
Monica Tanouye
Morgan Lyons
Moriah Haefner
MP Boardman
Nancy Chen
Nancy Jacobson
Nancy Oakes
Naomi Morauf
Nasiera Foflonker
Natalie Middleton
Nathalia Robbins-Cherry

Nathalie Teitler
Nathan McNamara
Nathan Weida
Nichola Smalley
Nicholas Brown
Nicholas Rutherford
Nick Chapman
Nick James
Nick Marshall
Nick Nelson & Rachel
  Eley
Nick Rushworth
Nick Sidwell
Nick Twemlow
Nicola Hart
Nicola Mira
Nicolas Sampson
Nicole Matteini
Nicoletta Asciuto
Niki Sammut
Nina Todorova
Niven Kumar
Norman Batchelor
Odilia Corneth
Olga Zilberbourg
Owen Williams
Paavan Buddhdev
Pamela Ritchie
Pankaj Mishra
Patrick Liptak
Patrick McGuinness
Paul Bangert
Paul Cray
Paul Ewing
Paul Gibson
Paul Jones
Paul Munday
Paul Myatt
Paul Nightingale
Paul Scott
Paul Segal
Paul Stuart
Paul Tran-Hoang
Paula Melendez
Pavlos Stavropoulos
Pawel Szeliga
Penelope Hewett Brown

Penelope Hewett-Brown
Peter Griffin
Peter Hayden
Peter Rowland
Peter Wells
Petra Hendrickson
Petra Stapp
Philip Herbert
Philip Leichauer
Philip Warren
Phillipa Clements
Phoebe Millerwhite
Piet Van Bockstal
Prakash Nayak
Rachael de Moravia
Rachael Williams
Rachel Andrews
Rachel Beddow
Rachel Belt
Rachel Carter
Rachel Darnley-Smith
Rachel Gaughan
Rachel Van Riel
Rahul Kanakia
Rajni Aldridge
Ralph Cowling
Ralph Jacobowitz
Rebecca Caldwell
Rebecca Carter
Rebecca Maddox
Rebecca Marriott
Rebecca Michel
Rebecca Moss
Rebecca Rushforth
Rebecca Shaak
Rebecca Surin
Rebekah Lattin-
    Rawstrone
Renee Thomas
Rhea Pokorny
Rhiannon Armstrong
Rich Sutherland
Richard Clark
Richard Dew
Richard Ellis
Richard Gwyn
Richard Ley-Hamilton

Richard Mansell
Richard Santos
Richard Shea
Richard Soundy
Richard Village
Rishi Dastidar
Rita Kaar
Rita Marrinson
Rita O'Brien
Robbie Matlock
Robert Gillett
Robert Hamilton
Robert Wolff
Robin McLean
Robin Taylor
Roger Ramsden
Ronan O'Shea
Rory Williamson
Rosabella Reeves
Rosalind May
Rosalind Ramsay
Rosanna Foster
Rosemary Horsewood
Royston Tester
Royston Tester
Roz Simpson
Rupert Ziziros
Ruth Curry
Ryan Day
Ryan Pierce
Sally Ayhan
Sally Baker
Sally Warner
Sally Warner
Sam Gordon
Samuel Crosby
Sara Bea
Sara Kittleson
Sara Unwin
Sarah Arboleda
Sarah Brewer
Sarah Lucas
Sarah Manvel
Sarah Stevns
Satyam Makoieva
Scott Chiddister
Sean Johnston

Sean Kottke
Sean McGivern
Selina Guinness
Severijn Hagemeijer
Shannon Knapp
Sharon Dilworth
Sharon Levy
Sharon McCammon
Sharon Rhodes
Shaun Whiteside
Sian Hannah
Sienna Kang
Silje Bergum Kinsten
Simak Ali
Simon Pitney
Simon Robertson
Simone Martelossi
Siriol Hugh-Jones
SK Grout
Sophie Nappert
Sophie Rees
Stacy Rodgers
Stefano Mula
Stephan Eggum
Stephanie Miller
Stephanie Smee
Stephanie Wasek
Stephen Eisenhammer
Stephen Fuller
Stephen Pearsall
Stephen Yates
Steve Chapman
Steve Clough
Steve Dearden
Steve Tuffnell
Steven Hess
Steven Norton
Stewart Eastham
Stuart Allen
Stuart Grey
Stuart Wilkinson
Sujani Reddy
Susan Edsall
Susan Ferguson
Susan Jaken
Susan Wachowski
Susan Winter

Suzanne Kirkham
Sylvie Zannier-Betts
Tania Hershman
Tara Roman
Tatjana Soli
Tatyana Reshetnik
Taylor Ball
Teresa Werner
Tess Cohen
Tess Lewis
Tess Lewis
Tessa Lang
The Mighty Douche
   Softball Team
Theo Voortman
Therese Oulton
Thom Keep
Thomas Alt
Thomas Campbell
Thomas Fritz

Thomas Noone
Thomas van den Bout
Thuy Dinh
Tiffany Lehr
Tim Kelly
Tina Rotherham-
   Winqvist
Tina Juul Møller
Toby Ryan
Tom Darby
Tom Doyle
Tom Franklin
Tom Gray
Tom Stafford
Tom Whatmore
Tracy Northup
Trevor Latimer
Trevor Wald
Trevor Brent Marta Berto
Tulta Behm

Turner Docherty
Val & Tom Flechtner
Val Challen
Valerie O'Riordan
Vanessa Dodd
Vanessa Heggie
Vanessa Nolan
Vanessa Rush
Victor Meadowcroft
Victoria Goodbody
Victoria Huggins
Vijay Pattisapu
Wendy Langridge
William Leibovici
William Orton
William Mackenzie
William Schwartz
William Wilson
Yana Ellis
Zachary Maricondia